"Come back," they said . . .
"WITH A GUN!"

He'd left this county because he'd killed a man—
and the dead man's brother had asked him to come
back—but to come back shooting!

Now he was back, back with his guns. He was back
in the county that meant nothing but trouble . . . not
fancy, worryin'-type trouble, but fists in the jaw and
death-dealing bullets.

Only—now that he was back in all this mess—he'd
found a girl who cared whether or not he cleared his
name . . . *and came through the range war alive!*

RANGE DRIFTER

Thomas Thompson

BANTAM BOOKS · LONDON · TORONTO · NEW YORK

All of the characters in this book are fictitious,
and any resemblance to actual persons, living or dead,
is purely coincidental.

RANGE DRIFTER

*A Bantam Book / published by arrangement with
Doubleday & Company, Inc.*

Bantam edition / March 1950
2nd printing .... March 1981

ISBN 0-553-14541-X

Published simultaneously in the United States and Canada

Bantam Books are published by Bantam Books, Inc. Its trademark, consisting of the words "Bantam Books" and the por-
trayal of a bantam, is Registered in U.S. Patent and Trademark
Office and in other countries. Marca Registrada. Bantam
Books, Inc., 666 Fifth Avenue, New York, New York 10103.

PRINTED IN THE UNITED STATES OF AMERICA

11 10 9 8 7 6 5 4 3 2

TO EMMA AND CHARLIE KING

1

HE AWOKE suddenly, as he always did, and his hand reached first for the gun he had placed under the blanket; a natural gesture. He rolled and sat up before he was fully awake and saw that it was Jean who was kneeling there beside him. Her face was close to his and he could see the worry. She said, "Bret's gone."

He felt an emotion that was more discomfort than anger and he knew it was because she had come to him first; she was making it his responsibility. He looked around quickly and saw that Sam was deep in his blankets. Maw would stay late in her bed in the wagon. Maw was sick, and they had had to stop often because of her spells. The fire was bright-flamed with new wood, and the coffeepot was curling thin fresh steam. Jean was fully dressed; when he looked at her the feeling of discomfort passed. He said, "The fence?"

She nodded. Her dark hair, done in two braids for the night, was as soft as the chilly dawn that was rumbling up out of the cap rock to the east. Her lips were full and inviting and her eyes, smudged from lack of sleep, could be bright with quick decision or soft with dreams. Ross Parnell had had a chance to see them both ways in the thirty days he had guided this Hedley family across the plains. He didn't like to think about it. It was no thought for a man who had come to rake up the coals of his past and accept a gun challenge. He rolled out of the blankets, fully clothed, and said, "How long ago did he leave?"

She had a way of accepting trouble calmly, as if she were used to it. "Fifteen minutes ago," she said. "I made him a pot of coffee and tried to talk him out of it. He told me to call Dad and get the wagon rolling. He thought we could cut the wire and be through before anyone saw us."

"As crazy as the rest of his decisions," Ross said, and he rubbed his knuckles, remembering yesterday.

She put her hand on his arm then and turned him toward her. There was no pretense about Jean Hedley, no toying of a woman's charms against a man's weakness. She said, "I don't blame you for the way you feel, Ross. But it's my family and it's all I have. Dad is beyond changing, I know, but Bret is young yet. It would kill Maw if anything happened to him. You know that. I want you to go after him, Ross."

He stood there in front of her, thinking of a dozen things he might say, saying none of them, somehow angry with her, angry with himself, impatient with the things that stood in his way. And he knew that this was the feeling that made him what he was, a drifter, and sometimes he wondered if perhaps the same feeling might not drive a man to doing things beyond his imagined capabilities. He didn't know. He said, "I'll go, Jean. For you. It might not be pretty to watch."

She nodded and pressed his arm. "I understand," she said.

He mounted his horse and rode toward the fence line of the XR where yesterday six men with rifles had turned them back on the Saboba road. To Sam Hedley who had stolen the mules that pulled the wagon the fence meant an obstacle in his way to the north breaks of the Sasinaw, where a man could steal the XR strays and build himself a herd. To Maw Hedley, with her failing heart, it meant another day away from a possible home. And to young Bret it was a flare of trouble that put a new light in his hazel eyes and stiffened him in his saddle.

But to Ross Parnell it had been more than that. It had meant meeting Trip Levitt face to face without making himself known. Trip Levitt who had spread the word up the cattle trails that if Ross Parnell ever came back to the Saboba country he had better come packing a gun.

Word that had spread and finally reached Ross in his constant drifting from one job to the next.

So Ross had come back, asking no favors and giving none; and yet on the way he had taken a responsibility that kept him from being a free man, for he had become a part of this Hedley family, and it was not by his own design.

At first the wagon and its occupants had been nothing more than an impersonal drag. He had hardly noticed the man who hired him, back there in Kansas; he had only heard that there was two hundred dollars in the job of guiding this family into the Saboba country and that had been enough. Ross wanted an excuse to go back, and he needed the money. It had been as simple as that.

But now, with the fence and those six riders who waited with rifles, it became a personal thing, and he was surprised to find that trouble across the road could make this difference. He refused to admit that this feeling was not sudden, but a thing that had come on him gradually without his wanting it. He had started out as a lone wolf, camping by himself within earshot of the wagon, showing them the way, giving answers when he was asked. And then near the end of the trip he realized that he would miss those rides with Jean and the dreamy half acceptance of reality that was Maw's. Even the flaring rebellion of old Sam, perhaps, and the constant gnawing trouble that was always in Bret. A man who was much alone could become a part of a family in thirty days of the confining proximity of the endless openness.

So he rode now to try to reason with Bret Hedley, when he should have been riding to accept the challenge of Trip Levitt. And somehow he was not sorry, and the gun felt good in the well-worn holster at his hip. There was a natural slant to the wide belt that circled his thin, muscle-tight middle. He wore a blue hickory shirt that was faded to a gray, sweat-streaked some. Around his neck was a yellow kerchief, the only touch of color. His shoulders sloped away from his neck and his arms were long. He wore no gloves, and his wrists, bony but small where they showed beneath the cuff of his too-short sleeves, were burned brown from the weather, a good match for his long-fingered hands.

Suddenly the sun came out of the cap rock, glaring across the land, and the land glared back—an unyielding land, a land of quick storm and sudden heat. A land of anger and violence and change. In the spring the drenching rains came and all winter the sky lay like a spongy mass of wet rawhide, molding itself across the flatness, watching the devil-knife of the blizzard howling its frenzy at the wind. Now the steady sun had come, a month early, and it might not stay, but for today the sky stood hot and brassy, puckered against the filmy horizon and bellied up tight and wind-parched above the fence and the wagon.

This was the domain of the XR, a land Ross knew well. Here he had grown to manhood and had dabbed his first loop on an XR calf and taken his first cussing from Tuck Brant himself. Here he had fallen in love with Lenore Brant, queen of these holdings; he had killed Vance Levitt because of her. And then he had drifted, never satisfied, never still, never knowing for sure what it was that made him wander an endless trail. Until word had come that Trip Levitt was here in the Saboba country and Trip Levitt was saying that what the law had called self-defense he called murder. Ross felt the muscles tighten along his jaws. Yesterday he had had a chance to ask Trip Levitt about that and he had kept still; yesterday he had thought first of the Hedleys.

The sun was soft and warm on his back as Ross rode toward the fence line. He thought of men digging post-holes in this baked and rocky soil, stringing wire while the sun burned the moisture from their souls, and he thought of men snaking up posts from the ice-toothed canyons while the blizzard howled its agonized hell on the lip of the plains. Then he thought of Bret Hedley and old Sam, rebels against progress and against society, and that old feeling of rebellion surged up within him, making him want to turn and ride his own way. The unmistakable ring of steel against steel reminded him of his promise to Jean, and he spurred his horse and rode toward where Bret Hedley worked with a single-bit ax and a light sledge against the top wire of the fence.

He pulled his horse to a sliding stop and threw himself from the saddle, hitting the ground on the run. Up the fence line, coming from the east, he had seen the six riders, and he had recognized the squat form of Trip Levitt. From the west, in the direction of the XR headquarters, two more riders were taking shape, heading for the fence, attracted, no doubt, by the smoke of the Hedley camp fire. He called a warning to Bret, and the kid turned, dropped the sledge, and stood there, the ax gripped in his right hand. Bret said, "Keep out of this, Parnell."

"You're being a damn fool, Bret," Ross said, trying to keep his voice calm. "I told you last night I'd talk them into letting us through. You cut that wire and all hell will break loose."

There was an open sneer on Bret Hedley's face. He said, "I feel the same way about you I did yesterday, Parnell. Take one more step and I'll let you have it with this ax!"

Ross fought down the anger that was in him and tried to reason. He said, "I know these people, Bret, and I know this country. I'm telling you you're making a mistake. Get away from that fence before I have to take you away."

"I'm waiting," Bret Hedley said. His shoulders had slouched and he drew the ax back in a half swing.

For a split second Ross stood there, poised on the balls of his feet, then he threw himself forward. The ax came down hard, the handle biting into his shoulder with a nerve-deadening crunch. He twisted and sunk his left elbow in Bret's stomach and heard the wind whistle out of the kid's lungs. He followed through quickly and locked his hands around the handle of the ax and twisted hard. He felt Bret's grip break, then the kid stepped back and drove his fist and it caught Ross high on the left cheek.

He hadn't wanted it to be this way, but there was no way of handling the kid sensibly. He caught himself wondering how he would explain to Jean, and then he let loose a short, vicious blow that caught Bret on the point of the chin. The kid went back, his hands shoulder high. He hit the fence and hung there for a second, and then his legs went out from under him and as he fell the barbs of the wire caught in his clothes and ripped his shirt, leaving a string of cloth on the second wire. Ross stepped forward and pulled Bret to his feet. Before he could move Trip Levitt and his men were there, their ponies' hoofs spurting white dust as they pulled to a stop. Levitt threw himself from the saddle, gun in hand. He said, "I told you to stay away from this fence."

Bret Hedley was starting to come around. Ross released his grip and the kid walked unsteadily and leaned against a post, wiping the blood from his mouth. Ross looked at Trip Levitt, and he calculated the distance between the wagon and the two riders from the ranch, who were coming up fast now. His brush with Bret had lighted the torch of anger and he wanted to have it out with Trip Levitt here and now so that it would be done. He bit off the words he wanted to say and said instead, "Personal argument, nothing more."

"Looks to me like one of you been beatin' on that fence

wire," Levitt said flatly, the gun in his hand tilting. "I told you you wasn't goin' through here."

"We'll go around it if need be," Ross Parnell said. "First I'll take my no from Tuck Brant himself."

Trip Levitt studied Ross a long time and he spit over his broad, flat chin. He said, "I reckon you'll have to go to hell to get it, then. Tuck Brant's been dead three years. His daughter runs the XR and it's her orders I'm givin' you."

It didn't make sense, standing here trying to reason with Trip Levitt. Although Trip had never seen the man who killed his kid brother it would be only a matter of time until he learned Ross's identity, and that would be all right with Ross. He thought of that now, but he thought more of Maw Hedley and of Jean. He looked at Bret, still leaning against the post, and he said, "I hired out to take these folks to Saboba. They want to pass through, nothing more. I'll promise they won't stay on XR land."

"The XR don't need your help to keep maverickers and wheat men off its land," Trip Levitt said. "This wire here does a good job." Then, pursing his lips and letting a crinkle form at the corner of his left eye, "Course now if you wanted through bad enough——"

Ross could see what was fermenting in Trip Levitt's mind. He could tell it by the way Levitt smacked his lips over his still-unspoken proposition and by the way he turned toward his men and winked, as if asking for approval of his plan. Ross said, "I might listen to reason."

Trip took his time. He said, "Well now, hard to say. That don't look much like an up-and-coming outfit you got there. Still, never can tell——" The men on the horses were grinning now. Trip holstered his gun.

"How much?" Ross said flatly.

"Well now," said Levitt, still toying with Ross's temper, "there's all the work of fixin' the fence. Costs money to keep good men like these on the job." He smacked his lips and made his decision. "Say, now, you had about fifty dollars and wanted to get through bad enough——"

Bret Hedley had pushed himself away from the post and stood there, feet spread, eyes blazing with hatred. "Damn you, Parnell!" he cursed. "So you're in with them, are you? I knew this was what it was leading to."

The name Parnell hung in the flat, dry air like a visible object, obvious as a dewdrop in a spider web, deadly as the spider itself. It seemed to reach out and touch every man in Levitt's group, and it settled and stayed with Trip himself. "Parnell," he said, and the name renewed the echoes of its first utterance.

So this was it. Ross no longer remembered the Hedleys. He forgot the fence. Now it was man to man on a personal score and there was no room for anything else in his mind. "That's right, Trip," he said. "Ross Parnell." His right hand seemed strangely comfortable and at ease.

Trip Levitt's eyes were round and staring. His lips didn't move when he spoke. He said, "I been hopin' you'd show up."

There was no quick blaze of guns—no darting of hands to holsters. Two men stood there, two men alone. The silence between them was the silence of the high plains and of death, and it was a silence that would have to settle before a move would be made. They were men who knew that a gun can kill, and they respected the knowledge. It would take a waver of an eyelid, an unexpected move of one of the horses—— There was no real hatred between them in this second, it was only the knowledge that soon one of them would die. They did not hear the two riders who had ridden up and slid their horses to a stop. They still looked at each other, still caught in the spell, even after the girl spoke.

Her voice was high with emotion, but even then it had

an underlying huskiness about it that seeped inside Ross and stirred up embers long dead. The second for death was gone now; it would have to come again later. Ignoring Trip Levitt, Ross turned and heard the girl's sharp, quick questions, brittle with authority. "Trip! What's going on here?"

It was Lenore Brant. She looked as Ross knew she would look, as he had seen her a dozen times in the embers of a solitary fire.

Trip Levitt, his voice worried, said, "More fence cutters, ma'am."

Ross Parnell was looking straight into the violet-blue eyes of Lenore Brant. He saw the recognition start first in the flush on her cheeks, spread into a smile on her lips. She said only his name. "Ross!" He tried to read into it something more than was there, something he had wanted to hear.

2

IN THIS moment Lenore Brant was dominant and the others became insignificant in her presence. At a distance of a hundred yards she might have been a man. She wore Levis and a sheepskin coat, and sat her saddle with the same rigid arrogance that had marked her father before her. Her hair was completely concealed under the broad-brim, flat-crowned hat, and her mouth was set, hard. She was the boss of the XR, as completely inseparable from the ranch as the sky is from the land. Yet the rough clothing could not hide the soft curves of her body, and the studied hardness could not conceal the violet-blue dreams in her eyes. She demanded answers without asking more questions, and the men backed down and left Trip Levitt to face her.

Levitt's eyes went from Lenore Brant to Ross Parnell.

and when they rested on Ross the smoldering fire was still there, the promise of trouble. He said, "I was just trying to do my job."

Ross said, "I didn't know you ran a toll road through here, Lenore. Fifty dollars is a mite high." It was the man who had ridden up with Lenore Brant who spoke and broke the tension.

He was a small man, small in bone and scant of flesh, yet strikingly handsome. There were high spots of color in his cheeks and his clothes fitted him too well. He had a tiny, close-trimmed mustache, and when he spoke there was the slightest hint of an accent in his voice. He said, "I've told you time and again, Levitt, that the law says a gate every three miles. This road can't be closed off. The wheat ranchers will be using it."

Trip Levitt turned a look of open disgust on the speaker. He spit over his chin and said, "I been takin' my orders from Tony Sellew."

The small man twisted stiffly in his saddle, flashed a quick look at Lenore Brant. Her voice was perfectly modulated now. She said, "Go draw your pay and get off the ranch, Levitt. I'm through with you."

She turned toward Ross, then, her chin tilted, a flashing, open challenge in her eyes. He could not tell whether she was proud or ashamed as she said, "Mr. Parnell, my husband, Herbert Warrington."

There was a dull void in Ross Parnell that made him feel as if the strength had gone from his arms. He looked at Herbert Warrington and thought he saw more color in the man's cheeks. He felt self-conscious before Warrington's poise as Lenore's husband extended his hand. Ross took it, a soft hand not marred by work or weather. He said, "Glad to know you, Mr. Warrington." He wondered if his emotion showed in his voice.

There might have been an embarrassing silence then except for Lenore. She had turned her attention to the

Hedley wagon, which was pulling up to the fence line. Ross noticed that young Bret was standing, hat in hand, his eyes openly admiring this woman who made the prairie a backdrop for her presence. Sam kicked his foot against the brake and hauled up noisily. He said, "I hope there ain't no trouble here. I got a sick woman." There was a pleading whine in his voice.

Lenore did not smile, and she let her gaze linger openly on young Bret. Bret colored slightly, and Ross felt a hard knot of jealousy in the pit of his stomach. She was the same as she had always been. Every man felt that intangible attraction the minute he looked at her. Men had fought over Lenore Brant. Ross had killed. Ross moved off and left Lenore and her husband with Sam Hedley and he didn't try to avoid his meeting with Trip Levitt. Levitt's voice was strained, as if his mouth might be dry. He said, "Another time, Parnell."

Ross nodded shortly. "I'll be watching my back," he said.

Levitt jerked his horse savagely, motioned to his men, and rode back up the fence line. Ross hunkered down, his back to a post, and made himself a cigarette. The shadow told him that a man was standing near him. He looked up and saw that it was Herbert Warrington.

There was something in Herbert Warrington of insignificance strangely at odds with power. He looked like a man who would go to great lengths to avoid trouble, and just as far to complete it once it was found. There was a polish about him that could have come only from an ancestry of culture and wealth. That was the part Lenore Brant had married, Ross caught himself thinking. Warrington smiled now, not a friendly smile. He said, "I won't pretend, Parnell. I've heard the story of you and my wife until I'm sick of it. They never say it to me openly, but it's always there, just the same. I've hated you in a way, I guess, but now that I've met you I don't. I wanted to say that and get it over with."

The impenetrable mask of the man's thin features was a thing that could be felt. Ross squirmed uneasily, groped for words, and said, "It was a long time ago. I forget the past. Why don't you do the same?"

The look was still there. Warrington said, "Some men can forget, and some men can't." He turned quickly and left; he seemed taller than Ross had thought. Ross twisted out the cigarette between his fingers, not feeling the burn.

Sam was introducing Maw Hedley to Lenore Warrington; and Ross could hear Maw saying, "It's awfully good seeing a woman out here, Miz Warrington. That means a heap to me, seeing a woman out here. Maybe we can be real good neighbors." Ross wondered if Lenore would answer; when she didn't, he knew she hadn't heard the offer of friendship. That was like her.

"I'm not in the habit of letting people through my fences," she said directly to Sam, "and I'm not in the habit of getting mixed up in these quarrels. But I do feel responsible for my man trying to charge you to go through, so in your case I'm going to make an exception."

"Now doggone if that ain't nice of you, Miz Warrington," old Sam whined. "All we want is to get to Saboba. Me, now, I'm a blacksmith, and I aim to open shop there. My wife here and my girl, they do sewin' mighty good and they figgered maybe they could take in a little."

Ross winced under the obvious lying of old Sam Hedley, knowing for sure that Lenore was seeing through the forced conversation. He felt an acute sense of embarrassment for Jean, and he caught himself looking toward the wagon to see how she was taking it. He couldn't see her, so he shifted his position some, then hunkered down in the shade of the wagon. It was there that Lenore found him. She said, "For an old friend you've had little to say."

He didn't look at her. "I said it a long time ago," he told her.

She laughed, that soft laugh that seemed to come from deep inside and reach out and touch a man, making him forget that she was a woman playing a man's role. She moved around to where he had to look at her and her precisely bowed lips were half smiling. He tried to take his gaze away, found he couldn't. He remembered those lips, not wanting to remember, and he remembered how those eyes could turn a smoky blue under the touch of dreams. She laughed at him. "Ross, I thought by now you would have grown up."

He fought a hopeless uneasiness, born of desires he was trying to keep down, not knowing what to say. The springs of the wagon complained slightly as Jean Hedley climbed out over the tailgate. It was not a task that could be accomplished with polished grace, and Lenore Warrington giggled at the awkwardness. With the amused lilt still in her voice she said, "Have you been hiding her, Ross?"

Ross introduced them clumsily, knowing that Jean had heard their conversation, knowing that Lenore knew it. There was still that half-taunting amusement in Lenore's voice. She said, "Why, you're just a child, aren't you?"

Jean Hedley said, "I'm not married, if that's what you mean." Ross felt his eyes widen, and a certain new evaluation of this girl came to him. Her voice natural now, Jean said, "I wanted to thank you for saying you'd let us through, and I wanted you to know that Mr. Parnell tried to keep my brother from cutting your fence."

"That's sweet of you to let me know about Ross," Lenore said, her voice flavoring the words. Then, "Your brother? He's the handsome one there?"

"He's just a child too," Jean Hedley said, and she turned and went around the wagon to where Sam was talking earnestly to Herbert Warrington.

"Well!" Lenore Warrington said. "Our kitten has claws! She'll be good for you, Ross."

He knew the temper of this woman. He had seen it in both her and her father. Again that knowledge that he could no longer think only of himself—that he must consider the Hedleys—came to him. He fought down the answer he would have liked to make and said instead, "I'm interested mostly in getting through that fence."

"Are you in love with her?"

He turned on her quickly, knowing that emotion was white in his face. He said, "Look, Lenore. The past is gone, see? I'll be in town two or three days, maybe, then I'm drifting on."

"After you meet Trip Levitt?"

"Maybe," he said.

She didn't laugh now. She said, "You'll kill again and drift again. You're not much of a man, Ross Parnell."

Nothing else she could have said would have stirred the feeling that that remark did. There was a primitive, savage instinct in him that made him want to take her in his arms and hold her until she was limp and helpless from the sheer strength that was in him. He turned quickly, knowing for sure now that his feeling for her was not gone, and went to where Sam and Herbert Warrington were watching Bret work on the first of the four wires.

He took the light sledge and single-bit ax from Bret savagely, without asking for them, and, catching the wire on the flat surface of the ax blade, he swung with the sledge. Twice more, and the wire parted with a snarling snap, slashing angrily and wrapping itself around the next post. In time he had cut all four strands, and stood there, perspiration drenching his shoulders, his exertion flaring his nostrils; he motioned for Sam to bring the wagon through. He saw that Herbert Warrington's eyes had never left him. Warrington said, "I suppose it takes muscles to do that?"

Lenore had mounted her horse and was looking at Ross, smiling. She said, "The main fence camp is there ahead a ways. Herbert will go along to explain that we let you through or you might run into trouble. I want to talk to you a minute, Ross."

He dropped his horse back alongside her. She said, "It's not the first time I've met rustlers in the guise of store-keepers and blacksmiths, Ross." Her voice was hard, metallic, and when he looked at her he saw that her mouth was ugly and straight. Her eyes seemed to be suddenly pale and hard, like the eyes of a cat about to spring on its prey. She spoke now with her lips tightly compressed against her teeth. "They shot Dad in the back when he tried to protect what was his."

Herbert Warrington was staring straight ahead. Ross said, "I'm sorry, Lenore. I didn't know about it."

She said, "That's why I called you back here to talk to you. We're fencing the XR, Ross. Every foot of it. We've got troubles enough without more maverickers moving in. Keep them moving."

She wheeled her horse and rode back toward the XR headquarters; when she was gone, the high charge of trouble and conflict seemed to leave the air. He looked at her once, and was conscious again that she was wearing Levis and a sheepskin coat. For just a second she seemed more man than woman. He turned his head and saw that Herbert Warrington was watching Lenore too.

3

HERBERT WARRINGTON wanted to talk, and Lenore's turn-ing back was like the removal of a cork from a bottle of effervescent liquid, capped too long. He talked with a reckless disregard of confidence, the talk of a man who has no friends, no one with whom he can pass more than a noncommittal remark on the weather. Ross listened, at times feeling almost a touch of friendship for the man, at times being acutely embarrassed.

He came from a well-to-do and prominent Boston family, Warrington said, and for the past five years, while Ross had been wandering, trying to lose himself, Warrington had been investing and losing the money that had been left to him. "I just haven't hit the right thing yet," he said with that almost childlike wistfulness that was a part of him.

"The XR is a mighty good spread," Ross said.

"For cows, you mean?" Warrington asked. "Are you another one who believes God made this country for cows and nothing else, and any man who says otherwise is an outlaw who should be hanged?"

"I hadn't thought of it that way," Ross said, hedging, "but maybe it's the way a cowman has to feel."

"But why the almighty cowman?" Warrington pressed, gesturing with his hand. "I've known men who had never seen a cow and they seemed to be normal and likable enough." He paused, looking off across the glaring sheet of plains, then added, "A damn sight more normal than most I've met here."

Ross grinned. "Funny talk for a man in the cow business, Mr. Warrington."

"I'm not in the cow business," Warrington said flatly. "That's one thing I can still say with a measure of pride."

Ross shifted uneasily in his saddle, not knowing what to expect next. He thought some of riding up and talking to Sam for a moment, but Herbert Warrington had ridden his horse closer, and now reached out and put his hand on Ross's arm. His eyes were bright, and he spoke like a man who has decided to lay his soul out on the table and look at it. He said, "The trouble with her, Parnell, is that she's always had what she wants. She saw a pasture once where she wanted to run her own string of horses. A little thing—thirty thousand acres of grass between Catclaw Creek and the escarpment—the richest land on the bench. She got it, and four farmers moved out. The XR still runs cows on that land, Parnell, and they've got no more right to it than they have to this wagon here." His face grew bitter and hard, and again Ross had the feeling that here was a man who would be hard to turn once he set his course. Warrington said, "Frankly, I'd as soon see her lose her precious XR as go on this way."

Ross tried to break the conversation again. He said, "I reckon the XR will be here when a lot of us are gone."

"What is the XR?" Warrington shot the question quickly, like a man who has suddenly, in a single phrase, found an unbeatable argument. "Answer that, Parnell. What is the XR?"

Ross hedged uneasily, pinned by the voice and eyes of this man who seemed, at times, verging on a self-imposed hysteria. Ross said, "The most successful cow outfit on the plains."

"You're avoiding the issue, Parnell," Warrington said quickly, reining his horse close. "You're like everyone else in this country. Do you want to know what the XR is? I'll tell you. It's more land than anyone has a right to own; it's land that no one owns. It's God knows how many tick-infested brutes that wander where they please. It's Tuck Brant and it's Lenore because Tuck came in here and stole what he wanted and passed it on to his daughter. It's a symbol without a purpose or a soul, and it will go on that way until somebody changes it. Those little ranches across the Sasinaw—Ed Tozier, Loop Fenton, Gib Baudry. Judge Iverson himself for all I know. They'll go on driving cows back and forth, fighting over stray calves, trying to stop us from fencing, getting themselves killed off. And the mighty XR will go on living and it will be Lenore Brant and Tony Sellew and cows. Have you ever thought what it would be like to be married to land and cows, Parnell?"

The little man's voice had risen to a pitch, like the voice of a man who has too much emotion locked up inside him. And for the first time Ross could understand Herbert Warrington, for Ross, too, had run from the idea of being married to an intangible. He coughed uneasily and said, "The XR won't change, Warrington."

"The hell it won't," Herbert Warrington said sharply, and now the full determination of the man was in his voice. "You saw the fence, didn't you?"

He had, Ross admitted, but what difference did it make? Maverickers had always preyed on the XR, just as they did on any open range of that extent. A fence would consolidate the holdings, make the XR more powerful. Warrington cut him short. He said softly, "Has there ever been mavericking on the south line, Parnell? That's unclaimed range for five hundred miles without a settler on it."

"I thought of that," Ross hedged. "I wondered why you bothered to fence that side."

"It's not a case of bothering," Warrington said. "It's a case of putting a fence where it will stay. The south plains aren't settled yet, but they will be. There's surface water under every inch of it. You'll see two or three windmills to the section, Parnell, and it will be my money that puts them there. That's wheatland, Parnell, the finest in the country, and you'll see every mile of it planted. Fence in the XR?" He laughed again, that quick, high laugh. "I don't care if the north side along the Sasinaw is ever fenced!"

Ross thought of the vastness of the table-flat land they had crossed after climbing the escarpment, and he tried to picture it a sea of wheat, green, rolling in the spring rains; golden and rich in the summer sun. He said only, "That won't change the XR, Warrington."

Warrington shook his head pityingly. "You can't see it, can you, Parnell? You're like her—you're like Tony Sellew. None of you have any time for change because you were raised on the pap Tuck Brant and land-grabbers like him fed you. The hell with what's inside a man. How many sections does he claim and how many cows does he run, that's the important thing. I hate the sight of a cow, Parnell. Every killing, every land grab, every burned-out home, every ripped-out fence in this country has been because of cows. Isn't it about time someone comes in here who can think of something besides cows?"

"It's cow country," Ross said stubbornly.

Warrington laughed. "Is it?" he said, taunting. "Talk to Ben Fransen there in the town. Oh, you'll meet him," Warrington hastened to assure, seeing Ross's questioning look. "Fransen is new here, but he's gone a long way. He's got money and he's got sense. Sense enough to find out that the benchland between the Catclaw and the escarpment is public land. Surprises you, doesn't it? Lenore's range, the little present for her horse pasture. There'll be settlers filing on that, too, and I'll finance them through their first wheat crop if necessary."

A stir of uneasiness ran through Ross as he thought of the vast reach that had always been claimed by the XR. It was no surprise to find that it was public land; it was surprising to find that anyone would settle there. He said, "You'll build yourself trouble, Warrington."

"You see?" Warrington said smugly. "I'll build trouble. Who am I? Only the legal owner of the XR, Parnell. That's all I am. But I can't do what I please with land I own. I can spend ten thousand dollars on fence, I can buy a dozen herd bulls, I can marry a Brant. But can I become the XR?" He shook his head. "Not me. Not as long as there are cows, Parnell. Not as long as there are cows."

"A rider yonder," Ross said, jerking his head, glad for

the interruption. This man was a fanatic of some kind. It worried Ross, being around him.

Warrington said, "Tony Sellew." He said it flatly, with disgust. "He's more of the XR than I am, Parnell. He knows cows. I can recite poetry to my wife, perhaps. Tony Sellew can talk cows. I promise you, Parnell, someday they'll have to talk wheat, and then it will be my turn. They can still call it the XR. People will, by habit. But it won't be Lenore Brant's XR; it will be Herbert Warrington's. I get a little tired of being Lenore Brant's husband. I had a name of my own, once."

Ross stared straight ahead, saying nothing. He didn't know this Tony Sellew who was riding out to meet them, but Warrington had made it clear Sellew was Lenore's right-hand man. The Brants had a way of finding men they could use. And once, a long time back, Warrington's reasoning wouldn't have sounded so strange, for once Ross Parnell had reasoned the same way. Lenore Brant could love a man, and she could love him violently, but as long as there was the XR she wouldn't. Ross had found it that way. Warrington said, "We have something in common, you and I and Sellew. We've all been in love with the same woman."

It was quick and unexpected, bitter. It left a bad taste in Ross Parnell's mouth. He looked at Warrington quickly, and saw the hard, set determination on the thin, pinched face, the fanatic gleam in the man's deep brown eyes. Ross bit off any answer he might have made.

The rider who came to meet them was about Ross's age. A tall, well-built man with the stamp of cows on him and the stamp of something more in the way he wore his gun and the lax, disjointed way in which he sat his saddle. He was dark and overly handsome, and he rode like a man who was born to the land and felt that he owned the land because of it.

Warrington's face had lost all its color. He sat stiffly in

the saddle now, and pointed with his chin. "There's another one, Parnell," he said. "A cowman. Even more of a cowman than old man Brant tried to make of his daughter. He talks cows and he eats and sleeps cows, and for all I know he thinks like a cow, and anyone who doesn't think likewise is fair bait to be hanged from a limb. But he doesn't see my wheat, Parnell, any more than you see it. He doesn't see wheat because it isn't cows."

And suddenly Ross saw that Warrington in his raving had not told as much truth as his eyes told now. It was Tony Sellew that bothered Lenore Brant's husband. His hatred of cows was only a figure.

But if Warrington hated his foreman, he didn't show it in the way he spoke. Rather, he spoke down to the man, and his voice had more of a snap than Ross had noticed before. He didn't bother to introduce the men, just said, "These folks are passing through. They're camping down in the breaks there tonight."

There was a slow insolence in the way Tony Sellew eyed Ross Parnell, the Hedleys, and the wagon. It was the age-old look of the horseman sneering down at inferior creatures who made a living from the soil. He dismissed Sam, his wife, and the wagon with a glance, and gave more time to young Bret and especially to Ross Parnell. He said, "I don't like nesters camping on the XR. The grass is dry now. Too much chance of fire. The road is good from the breaks on in. It won't hurt you to get to Saboba after dark."

There was a smile of absolute pleasure on Herbert Warrington's face. He said, "I didn't introduce you two, did I? Tony Sellew, this is Ross Parnell. He and his wagon are camping in the draw there tonight."

Tony Sellew kept a poker face. He had caught the full implication of the introduction, but he didn't show it. He shrugged his shoulders and said, "You're the boss," and without changing his voice or changing the expression on his face he put a lot of mockery into those words. Warrington caught it, and flushed deeply. To Ross, Tony Sellew said, "I'd advise against it." There was something in his eyes that was neither a threat nor a warning; rather it was an amused tolerance.

Ross didn't waver under the steady gaze of those pit-black eyes. He said, "I wasn't asking for advice."

Tony Sellew smiled. It was a smile that crinkled the corners of his eyes but didn't touch the eyes themselves. He said, "Sometimes you get advice without asking for it." He turned and rode his horse back to where more than twenty men were camped in a low swale that cut across the prairie. A dozen wagons stood there, some of them high with oak posts that must have been hauled for miles. Beyond the wagons was a stack of barbed wire, rolls and rolls of it, on stubby reels, each roll with two boards nailed in an "X" across each end. There was a cook wagon beyond that, and, in a rope corral, twenty or thirty mules and as many saddle horses.

"It's backfiring on him already," Herbert Warrington said softly. "He says his crew should be out chasing cows, and she makes him stretch wire. She'll never get him to build that north fence." He laughed, then, and the poise that Ross had noticed when he first met the man suddenly returned. He said, "It's been nice knowing you, Parnell. For your sake I hope you're just passing through; nasty disposition, that Levitt. If your friends there are interested in raising wheat, have them look me up."

He turned and rode back in the direction they had come, a strange, small man who did not look well on the back of a horse. A man, Ross knew now, who was heartbreakingly alone in a place where he didn't fit. Somehow it occurred to Ross that there was a mighty thin line between love and hate. Someday soon Herbert Warrington was going to decide which side of that line he was on.

Ross rode forward and told Sam to keep the wagon

clear of the fence camp. There in the rim of the distance they could see the green line that marked the break they were seeking.

They rode in silence, watching the fence camp without seeming to watch, and for the first time in days Bret Hedley had nothing to say. It was hard to tell what he was thinking when he was silent like that.

The afternoon sun slanted in on them as they rolled across the grassland, the wagon tilting and bumping, the cover flapping listlessly. Once Jean put her head through the puckered opening at the tail gate of the wagon, saw Ross, and smiled. Ross grinned back, not knowing why he was grinning.

In time they found the stream, rimmed with willows, meandering through a grassy plot of land no bigger than a man's back yard. But the trickle of years had cut a narrow gorge through the lip of the benchland, and in this protected pocket a dozen cottonwoods grew to a good height. It was a natural spot for a camp, and Ross didn't bother to explore it.

He rode back, calculating the angle of descent down the steep bank. He told Sam to let the women out. Then, taking his lariat from his saddle, he dismounted and made the rope fast to the rear axle. "Better put a little drag on her," he explained to Sam. "She's steeper than she looks."

Jean and her mother had found the narrow trail made by cows on their way to water. The women were already near the bottom of the bank. Jean was exclaiming about the trees like a six-year-old with a new doll, and Ross liked the sound of it. There was a sort of warmth and goodness to her childishness.

"That hoss of yours hold all right, Bret?" Ross asked. There was nothing unfriendly about his tone of voice.

"None better," Bret said.

The feeling of trouble that was past and the prospects of the first good camp in a week had touched all of them.

"Take a dally around your horn and pull him back," Ross directed. "I'll dig in my heels on this other rope and hold him from turning over when he hits that slide there at the bottom. Keep your brake set, Sam. She'll take it all right."

It was no trick to get the wagon down. Rubbing the slight rope burn in the palm of his hand, Ross coiled the lariat and started looking around for a camp site. Sam got down from the wagon and stood there, flexing his legs and shoulders. He said, "They know damn well they ain't got no right to fence, or they wouldn't have give in so easy."

Maw Hedley, as methodical as a machine, had already started to unpack the cooking utensils and bedding. Jean, apparently, had gone exploring into the shade of the narrow gorge. The silence of being busy spread from the little group and hung in the hot, flat air. Because of that silence Jean Hedley's scream was twice as horrible.

Only instinct could have made Ross Parnell move as quickly as he moved now. With one lunge he shoved Maw Hedley behind the wagon and then he was running up the cottonwood-shaded gorge, his gun in his hand.

He found Jean standing near one of the big trees, both hands pressed tightly over her mouth. She didn't look around when he called her name. She just screamed again in that piercing, high note of terror that rippled the skin on a man's back. Then she started to sway, and he caught her in his arms and held her face against his shoulder. Slowly his eyes went to the tree.

The thing that was turning there at the end of the rope had been a man once. Now it was a slack, loose-jointed object that hung dejectedly, its head dropped on its chest. It turned more, and Ross could see the face, discolored and distorted, the tongue protruding. He felt suddenly sick to his stomach.

He picked Jean up in his arms and carried her back

toward the wagon and he saw Sam and the others standing there by the stream near a clump of willow. There
was another person with them, a woman, about Maw
Hedley's age. She was sitting on a rock, and Maw had her
arms around the woman's shoulders and was sort of rocking her back and forth, as a mother might rock a child.

Ross could hear the woman's dry, racking sobs, hear
her saying, "They hung my husband. He didn't do nothin' a hundred other men ain't done before him, but they
hung him anyway. Damn their souls to hell!"

Standing there, holding Jean in his arms, Ross looked
from one to the other. The hard brightness of eyes and
the flush of excitement were on the face of young Bret
Hedley. Old Sam's cheeks had sucked in until they looked
like pockets in a puckered piece of canvas. Most of the
vacantness was gone from Maw Hedley's face. She stroked
the other woman's forehead and said, "There, there,
now. We'll take care of you."

Old Sam said, "It's time somebody put a stop to their
high-handedness and their damn fencin'. We got the law
on our side now. Enough of us get together we can do it.
That's what it takes, ma'am, all of us pullin' together."

"And show 'em we ain't afraid of nothing." It was
Bret. He had drawn his gun and he was looking at it
with those hard, bright eyes of his.

Jean opened her eyes, then buried her face deeper into
Ross Parnell's shoulder. He didn't realize that his arm
had suddenly tightened around her, holding her close,
as if he were trying to protect her.

4

THERE WAS little sleep that night in the small canyon,
for the presence of the dead man was there, touching

each of them as surely as if in death he had become an integral part of their lives.

Only once had the dead man's wife noticed Ross, and then she had looked at him for a long time with those red-rimmed, hard, tear-glazed eyes, and there was recognition dulled with grief; but she said nothing. It had been a long time since Ross had seen Loop Fenton, the rustler, and now Loop Fenton was dead, and his wife sat there and stared into the embers of the fire, and Maw Hedley whispered to her and pulled a shawl tighter around the woman's bony shoulders.

Once Ross thought of going to Jean and talking to her. He could tell her that this was a raw and untamed land where a man's law was what he thought was right or wrong. But he was afraid he could not make her understand. The argument would be weighted on the side of the dead man, for death has a way of outbalancing reason with emotion.

So he kept to himself. The night came first to the canyon and then spread softly blue over the vast expanse of the plains. The night was unchecked by Lenore Warrington's fence, and the guns of Tony Sellew and Trip Levitt could not stop it. Like the night, bits of the past came unchecked and unbidden to Ross Parnell: some of those bits he was able to expel from his mind as easily as he expelled the blue cigarette smoke from his nostrils, but other bits stayed there, probing at his memory, driving a surging uneasiness through his body, leaving a weariness in his brain.

By the fire he could see the Hedleys and Agnes Fenton, the wife of the dead rustler. They were having coffee now, and were talking earnestly; it occurred to Ross that Agnes Fenton was becoming a part of this Hedley family, just as he had become a part of it. Yet it was different, and it bothered him.

It was not a fear of anything Agnes Fenton could say

—there were a hundred people in Saboba who could say the same thing. But rather it was a fear of what this woman's emotion could do to the Hedleys. Sam Hedley had come to Saboba to steal cows and build a herd. It was his admitted intention, and in his way he considered it right and just that he should get his start in a new land in this way. Others had done it before, and some of them had become powerful and respected names in the state. But that was twenty years back, when a man drove cows with one hand and fought Indians with the other—when the very magnitude of his isolation sanctioned his creed of survival of the fittest. Now there was civilization here on the high plains, and there was the fence.

In a strange, detached way Ross had come to like Sam, could have liked him completely except for the rank dishonesty that stood like a canker in every move Sam made. Outside of that there was the basic goodness and the basic meanness that could be found in any man. But Sam was willful and headstrong, and in his pale blue eyes there was a smoldering hurt that said he had been stepped on by men bigger than himself. Perhaps it was this that made him want to maverick and steal from men who could afford to lose, and in such stealing he found nothing to disturb his conscience. Tonight, with a dead husband as an ally, Agnes Fenton would have no trouble convincing Sam Hedley that his thinking was right. Ross stirred uneasily and wished suddenly that he had taken the time to find out how Jean felt about these things.

They broke camp early, a silent, stony-faced group with little to say and much to think about. Twice, now, Agnes Fenton had called Ross by name—once when he offered to pour her more coffee, and again when he took the shovel from the wagon and started up the draw. She said then, "I won't stand for my man being buried on XR range, Ross. Sam and Laura, here, said I could take him into town and bury him decent, like he deserves."

Young Bret gripped his coffee cup tightly in both hands and blew across the scalding liquid. Without raising his eyes he said, "Maybe Ross figures a man's soul could rest on ground that's claimed by murderers. We don't see it that way."

Ross let it go. This was no time to start an argument.

They changed off sometimes to break the monotony, Bret riding on the seat alongside Sam, Maw inside the wagon, and Jean, in divided skirt, riding Bret's chestnut gelding. Without knowing, or stopping to consider why, Ross had come to look forward to these shifts, for when Jean rode the gelding she was apt to keep close to him, and the time went fast, hurried along by her constant questions and her exuberance over things inconsequential. Yet when Ross saw that this was to be the arrangement this morning he did not feel the sudden lift he had come to expect. Today there would be no whispered awe at the looming mass of the towering escarpment, no sharp exclamation at the unexplainable table-flat mesas that appeared from nowhere, no warm and friendly mock irritation at Ross's stock explanation that every new piece of vegetation was just a weed.

There would be other questions today, he knew, for Jean Hedley, in spite of her youth and her unpracticed nonchalance, was a woman, and a woman is inquisitive. They rode a long time in silence, and then she said what he knew she would say; he had been expecting it all morning, and still it caught him off guard. "I didn't know you had worked for the XR."

He waited awhile before he answered, reining his horse slightly to the left, out of the wagon dust, feeling the steady muscular flow of the animal beneath his thighs. He said, "If a man worked at all, he worked for the XR."

"There was Loop Fenton and others."

So Agnes Fenton had spread her poison, and, even after Loop was dead, she had gone on with the ancient campaign of winning new recruits in the decade-old war of the plains—the little man against the big man. If she had gone this far, she had gone further, and perhaps she had told of the night when XR punchers had caught four rustlers red-handed and had dealt with them by the only law that was then known on the plains. Ross looked at the girl, and he held her with his eyes as he said, "A man decides what is right and wrong."

Her open appraisal of him did not waver, and he became acutely conscious of the turn of her lips and the deep beauty of her eyes and the soft, full contour of her body. She said, "Does a man decide, or does he let a woman decide for him?"

He shrugged, and thought of a time when he had tried to make that same decision for himself; he realized now that he had been trying to make that decision during these years that he had been away. It was unfair to say that he had been motivated completely by the charms of Lenore Brant. He had convinced himself of this, and yet when he had seen her there at the fence line the stinging emotion laced him like salt water in an open sore and there had been nothing he could do about it. He felt a sharp annoyance, and he said abruptly, "We'll be in Saboba by noon."

She rode with her head turned to one side, her eyes on his face, studying him as if trying to see the workings of his mind; he somehow felt that he owed her an explanation, yet there was no explanation to give, nor was there anything for which he need be ashamed. She asked, "You'll go back to the XR?"

It was none of her affair, yet he didn't mind her asking. In a way, he was warmly pleased at her interest. He shook his head. "I haven't made any plans."

Again she gave him that close scrutiny. She said, "Do you ever, Ross?"

It was a direct question, deserving a direct answer. He

looked at her and smiled a little. "No," he said. He was glad that she did not play the woman and preach a sermon.

She said, "Is it because you still have ideas of what's right and wrong?"

"Doesn't any man?" he asked.

She rode her horse close to his and she shifted the reins to her right hand and put her left hand out toward him. He took the small, well-shaped palm with his right hand, and the horses slowed; and they rode that way for some time, saying nothing. And then, softly, as if to herself, she said, "I'm sorry it's over, Ross." He was left to put his own interpretation on that statement, and he chose to believe it was the trip she was talking about.

There had been nothing personal between them except that during the past week they had become acutely conscious of each other; nothing more. Now he felt a sudden void as he realized that within a matter of an hour this association would be ended. It was strange that in that moment he should think so strongly of Trip Levitt and of Tony Sellew and of Lenore Warrington and of the strange, warped little fanatic who was Lenore's husband. He said, rather gruffly, "I'll be seeing you again before I leave town."

She let her fingers tighten around his large bony hand and she said, "Have you any advice to offer, Ross?"

He did have, and he told her: "Herbert Warrington said that if you are interested in planting wheat, you should talk to him. If you want to run cattle, there's a man in town they call Judge Iverson. He's had a small spread here since the beginning, and you can trust his judgment. He's never had trouble with the XR because he owns his land and he buys his cows." He let his voice trail off.

She prompted him. "If Dad decides that his idea is best?"

Ross Parnell freed his hand of her grip and he looked straight ahead between his horse's ears. She was a girl who had sense and could take straight answers. He said, "There have always been some here who figured that way, Jean. Loop Fenton was one of them."

She said, "Thanks, Ross." He thought she was going to leave it at that, but she did the completely unexpected. With no touch of malice she said. "I feel sorry for Lenore Warrington."

He said, "Why?" He said it quickly, surprised. He had never thought of anyone feeling sorry for Lenore.

She said, "Because she's trying to be a man when she wants to be a woman. She's in love with her husband and doesn't know what to do about it."

She turned her horse and rode to the other side of the wagon and Ross was thoughtful, thinking of what she had said.

5

Noon was hot on the town of Saboba when they crossed the bridge that spanned the Sasinaw and led to the main street. The dust was deep, and the few horses at the hitch rails did not disturb it as they stood there listlessly, switching at flies.

It was a town with the mark of thwarted ambition about it. Once it had been the crossroad of cattle trails heading north and east to Dodge; then the trails had veered to meet the railroad, and the town had hung in a state of half-animation until live-wire speculators had decided the railroad should come here to this very place, making Saboba not a trail crossing but a trail terminus. New blood had stirred in the veins of the dying town, and it had grown beyond its bounds. Lumber, hauled

two hundred miles, spread its bright new glare around
the original thick-walled adobes.

But the railroad had not come to Saboba, and now,
again, the town was dying. Like a sick old man who
knows he has lost his chance, Saboba lay in the sun and
dreamed and growled at anything new that dared disturb
its slumber. It was growling now at the white-topped
wagons that came regularly with plows and cookstoves,
and hatchet-faced women and too many kids, and seed
wheat. It was growling, too, at the teamsters and the
strings of wagons that hauled tons of wire and staples to
the long warehouses down by the river. Wire and staples
for the XR fence, which, some men said, would someday
encircle the town and strangle out its last chance of life.

But there were others who saw in the coming of the
fence and the settling of the land a new era for the fer-
tile valley out by the Sasinaw River, slashing its aimless
and slow-moving way across the plains. Such men saw
in this country a land of such vastness that the XR, the
little cattlemen, and even the farmer would have room
to live and still not rub elbows. As long as ten years ago
Judge Iverson, who bore his title both by virtue of respect due him and his legal standing, had seen the land
this way and he had talked of it to Ross Parnell—a likable young waddy with dreams in his eyes who rode the
unfenced and unmapped domain of the huge XR. It was
of Judge Iverson that Ross thought now as he and the
Hedleys came into the sleepy, half-alive town.

If any man could be called the father of the Sasinaw
Valley it was Judge Iverson himself, for it was to the
judge the town of Saboba owed its life. Arriving in this
land of flat plain, sheltered valley, and tree-choked breaks
as far back as Tuck Brant himself had arrived, Judge
Iverson had stayed to plant a town. While Tuck Brant
blustered and pushed his way south into the plains, the
judge claimed a scant ten sections north of the river, and

bought his first herd. A good cowman, he nevertheless longed for neighbors and men to share the blessings of this new land, and he laughed at Brant, who set a new bride in the middle of a half a million acres of grass and complained he was crowded.

Out of his own ranch the judge carved a town site and in time others came to take up spreads that were infinitesimally small when compared to the unfenced domain of Tuck Brant, their powerful neighbor south of the Sasinaw.

Ed Tozier was first, claiming eight sections to the east of the judge. A complaining old man with a yoke of hard luck; a man, some said, who branded a few of the XR strays that dodged the weather in the Sasinaw breaks.

Gib Baudry, then, on the other side, and Gib Baudry's calf crop grew faster than was reasonable. Beyond Ed Tozier, other ranches came into being, and in time the cowboys of the XR started watching the unfenced line that edged along the Sasinaw.

Ross Parnell had been young. He saw them come and watched Saboba grow, and in time he himself was of saddle age and went to work for the XR. He heard talk then of maverickers and he came to know men like Loop Fenton—men who no longer bothered to take up land; men who made a living off XR beef.

In time there was war between men who had once been neighbors; through it all Judge Iverson stood firm and unyielding, not taking sides, running his ranch and nursing his town, which was a brawling youngster now with a reputation that was carried up and down the cattle trails that came here and crossed.

Impressionable, a dreamer of sorts, Ross turned to Judge Iverson on one hand and to Tuck Brant on the other; there was little in common between the two. Then the thing over which he had no control: Lenore Brant had been a girl who lived with her father; a sudden touching of eyes, and she was everywhere and she was everything. He could still hear Tuck Brant's booming voice, loud enough so that every man in the XR bunkhouse could hear. "What the hell you got to offer, you young pup? By God, I've only started to grow, and what's mine is my daughter's. What the hell you got to offer?"

As final as that, and the cold water of words quenched the embers of a dream. He was young, and a young man can make mistakes. He gambled some; he drank a lot. And then that night at Jim East's saloon when Vance Levitt had ridden in with trouble in his craw. Young Vance Levitt had said too much that night; young Vance had died. And now Ross was back, for Trip Levitt had come to make something of a five-year-old fight.

The town had changed little, Ross saw, in the time he had been away. Jim East's saloon was still at the main intersection, cool, quiet, and inviting. Inside those walls a man could drink with his friends or, remembering one night a long time back, a man could fight with his enemies.

The long, sprawling mercantile store was there, as was the butcher shop, where Loop Fenton and his kind had been able to sell a skinned beef with no questions asked. The frame buildings around the edge of town had not been there before, but now they were deserted, and already the weeds and the brush were creeping in claiming them again for the land.

Beyond the muddy creek that joined the river were the squat, squalid shacks of Hogtown, where a puncher, tired of the range, could spend his money in the numerous and ancient ways devised for such occasions.

And, it seemed, a new name had appeared in Saboba —Ben Fransen, Licensed Surveyor, Land Locator, and Dealer in Real Estate Loans. Ross Parnell looked at the gaudy cloth signs that covered the building and drew his mental picture of the man inside. It was strange that a land locator could do so well in the dying town of Saboba. He thought of Warrington and his wheatland between the Catclaw and the escarpment.

It was good to be back; for Ross there could have been more pleasure in it except for the fact that each person was too acutely conscious of the body of Loop Fenton wrapped in blankets there in the back of the wagon. All morning death had traveled with them and laid its pall of uneasiness over each of them and over the land they crossed. Now it reached out and touched the town and seemed to smother everything with an unreal gray silence. Ross rode close to the wagon, and to Sam Hedley he said, "The undertaker is there in the furniture store. We'd best take care of that first."

"It's the decent thing to do," Sam Hedley said.

Young Bret stared straight ahead. He said, "Damned bloody murderers."

And, although he himself felt no respect for the dead man, Ross removed his hat when he and Bret carried the blanket-shrouded figure into the store and followed the undertaker's directions that led them to the black-curtained, half-lit room there in back.

The renewed wailing of Agnes Fenton was a thing that went through Ross like a knife and drove him back out into the sunlight. Maw Hedley went into the little room with Agnes, and Ross stood close to Jean, there by the wagon; neither of them said anything. In time Maw Hedley and Agnes came out and got into the wagon, and Ross felt a twinge of irritation. He had not counted on Agnes Fenton going with them any farther. He had imagined she would stay there with the undertaker and the body of her husband.

But a man cannot reason with a woman's grief, so he mounted and led the way two blocks up the street and one block over to the left where the comfortable, long town house of Judge Iverson, the gaunt, gray-haired, soft-spoken owner of the JI Cross, hid in its cluster of cottonwood.

Ross dismounted at the familiar picket fence and went up the hollyhock-lined walk, knocking at the front door. The judge opened the door and stood there, a soft glow of pleasure on his face and no surprise in his eyes.

There was a tall, courtly dignity about Judge Iverson. It was augmented by his long, black broadcloth coat, which he wore even though the day was warm, and it was finished off by the flowing black tie that accented the whiteness of his neatly trimmed Vandyke. His eyes were the clear blue of a late fall sky, and his skin had a natural ruddiness. He extended both hands to his caller, then pulled Ross forward and stood there looking at him, like a father who has not seen his son for a long time.

The judge spoke softly and directly, as he always did. "I knew you were coming, Ross. Trip Levitt was in town last night. He did a lot of talking, and the sheriff and I decided the town would be better off without him. We sent him about his business and asked him not to come back."

"You didn't need to do that, judge."

"Things have changed a lot," the judge said. He had a way of laying down an ultimatum while seemingly engaged in casual conversation. He was doing that now. "Men don't go around shooting each other down on the streets." He hardly seemed to notice the gun on Ross Parnell's hip but he said, "There's an ordinance against wearing a gun in town."

Ross flushed deeply and the judge clapped him affectionately on the shoulder. "Enough of that," he said. "I hear you bring folks who want to settle here. We can use them, Ross. We need them. Saboba is not dead by a long shot, I'll tell you, and if it is to live we need new blood—new blood that will take the land and put down roots. We're living on a false bubble now, what with the fence crews and the wheat and the windmill builders. When that's done with, we'll need solid people who own their homes and have kids to send to school." He laughed heartily and said, "Just a town boomer at heart, eh, Ross? Get on in there, and let old Maria have a look at you so she can get her cry out. I'll go show your friends where to put their team. Past noon, and I'll wager you haven't had dinner yet." Conversation bubbled out of the man as if he were abundantly full of life.

Ross stood there and watched the old man stride down the walk, the tall, full-flowing dignity of him touching everything around. And he forgot the talk of fences and forgot the XR, but could not forget Trip Levitt. He was disturbed and uneasy about the judge taking a hand in things, but as long as he was in Saboba he would respect the judge's laws and decisions. He always had. There was a wide expanse out there beyond where no man made the rules.

He heard a quick cry of joy, and turned and saw Maria, a short, squat olive of a woman who had been the judge's housekeeper as long back as Ross could remember. The woman broke into an unintelligible stream of Spanish, then threw both arms around Ross's middle, hugged him tightly, and cried copiously. He grinned and said, "Now there, is that any way to greet your *pelado?*"

She pushed him away roughly and stepped back, deep indignation stamped on her moonlike features. "Pelado!" she repeated. "You are no pelado. You are the very best——"

They both started to laugh. It was a joke they had had between them—this business of Ross calling himself a pelado, a useless thing. It had always brought Maria stanchly to his defense.

She had to show him the kitchen first. The judge had bought her a new cookstove. And then there was the new bed that was sent all the way from Kansas City. And

there was this and there was that—things of no interest
and of no importance and Ross was anxious to get out to
help the Hedleys. But he examined each object carefully
and exclaimed over them, confirming Maria's constant
contention that there was nothing so fine in all *Los Es-
tados Unidos.*

The front door opened and closed and Ross pinched
Maria's cheek and went back into the parlor, leaving the
Mexican woman standing there, both hands on her hips,
looking after him adoringly.

The judge stood by the door a second, and then he
sank down into the nearest chair. He looked old and
tired. Ross felt a quick twinge of apprehension. He said,
"Are the folks putting the stock up?"

"Not here," the judge said softly. "Over in Loop Fenton's shack in Hogtown."

Ross said slowly, "I should have told you how come
Mrs. Fenton is with them. The canyon over there where
Coyote Creek cuts over the bench—— We found Loop
hanging by his neck. Looks like the XRs caught him
once too often. Agnes had got there before we showed
up. It was the only decent thing to do, Judge. The Hedleys didn't know Loop and had no part of him."

The judge looked helplessly at Ross Parnell, and on
his face was the look of a man who is thwarted from living by his own decisions. He said simply, "Trouble is
as close as that, Ross. I've been able to keep a few cool
heads hereabouts. If I were to take Loop Fenton's widow
in——" He stopped, embarrassed at his own inadequacy,
a man unused to making excuses for himself. He said, "I'll
get to the Hedleys later and have a talk with them, Ross.
Before Ben Fransen gets hold of them and starts putting
ideas in their heads. There's still school land over east
of Gib Baudry."

There were a dozen questions Ross wanted to ask, but
he was stopped from it by a heavy-knuckled pounding

on the front door. The judge got up slowly, inched the curtain back, peered out, then opened the door. A thick, stocky, black-bearded bull of a man stood there, his face hard-set, his eyes whisky-muddy. He was backed up by five other men whom Ross recognized as old-time small ranchers who had been here in the valley north of the Sasinaw as long as he could remember. He was surprised to see them led by this hulking block-faced man, for Gib Baudry was not a man to be picked for a leader.

Baudry was a hard-drinking, hard-fighting man, with a wolf-like temper that flared without reason. He was generally conceded to be a good man to leave alone. That temper of his was near the surface now and he spoke to the judge without any respect in his voice. Ross saw that the other ranchers shifted as if embarrassed.

Gib Baudry said, "You hear about Loop Fenton?"

"Yes," the judge said slowly. "Ross Parnell here and his wagon outfit brought him in. You remember Ross Parnell, don't you, boys?"

There was a mumbled and confused acknowledgment of the introduction from everyone except Gib Baudry. Baudry said, "What the hell you gonna do about it, Judge?"

Judge Iverson spoke carefully. "You know Loop's reputation, boys. We knew it would happen."

Gib Baudry broke in sharply. "Loop ain't stole a cow since we all had that talk with him. He said he was comin' in as one of us and he did. He was all through with maverickin' and you know it. He was ridin' across there mindin' his own business and Tony Sellew and his gunhawks jumped him and strung him up. You ever hear of anybody trying to steal a beef on Coyote Creek, smack in the middle of the XR? It ain't safe around here for no man now lessen he's an XR man, Judge, and by God——"

"Hold on a minute, Baudry," Ross Parnell broke in

softly. "All you've got to go on is what Loop's woman told you."

Gib Baudry looked at Ross Parnell directly for the first time. His muddy eyes crept slowly from the crown of Ross's head to the tips of his dusty boots, then went back and rested on the gun on Ross's hip. He said, "You back workin' for the XR, Parnell?"

"I just pulled into town," Ross said, "I'm only saying I saw Agnes Fenton and I know how she was talking. I don't think a man should take that kind of talk as gospel."

"Let's cool off, Baudry." It was old Ed Tozier, the judge's neighbor to the west. He was slight, trouble-bent. He said, "Hell, I got grief enough without startin' a war over nothing. There's a lot to what Parnell says."

Gib Baudry turned viciously on Tozier and slapped the old man hard across the face. Tozier, too startled to strike back, fell back and stood there, rubbing his jaw. Half-turned, covering the men behind him, filling the door with his huge bulk, Baudry shouted, "You and your damn bellyaching! What the hell you expect Ross Parnell to say, you fools! If he ain't workin' for the XR how come he can stand there with a gun hangin' on him when nobody else can? You forgettin' he was so damn sweet on that Lenore Brant bitch that he killed a man for her?"

6

So IT WAS back again, just the way he had left it, and the years had been unable to change it. For a long minute Ross stood there, looking into the glowering face of Gib Baudry, and slowly he unbuckled his gun belt and let it drop to the floor of the porch. He smiled some, and said, "You didn't mean that, did you, Gib?"

Gib Baudry's lips worked loosely. He started to curse, then lunged forward, and the heel of his fist caught Ross a glancing blow on the side of the head. Ross lashed out, his fist sinking deep into Baudry's paunchy middle, jack-knifing the man with pain. Ross hit again, his knuckles catching Baudry flat on the face, straightening him. Baudry's face was white except for the smear of blood that spouted from his nostrils. He began to cough and retch, violently sick. He staggered back down the steps and Ross followed him, hitting him again. The men moved aside, not offering to help him, Ross stood there, rubbing his knuckles. He said, "I brought a wagon here, nothing more."

The men might have answered, made apologies as men do, but a horse and rider had drawn up by the judge's front gate, a horse that champed nervously on a silver bit, a horse whose muscles sent a creaking through the heavy hand-carved saddle. Seemingly a part of the animal was Tony Sellew, leaning forward now, his hands on the broad saddle horn, his hat pushed back slightly from his dark, curly hair, a broad, pleased smile on his handsome face. He spit out the brown paper cigarette that was dangling from one corner of his mouth and said, "That was nice work, Parnell."

Ross looked at the foreman of the XR and the sharp dislike he had felt for the man before renewed itself. He said, "I wasn't looking for compliments, Sellew."

The smile never left Sellew's face. "You wasn't looking for advice yesterday, either."

"We made out all right," Ross said flatly.

Sellew laughed and straightened in the saddle. "They tell me you're a good hand, Parnell. Hard to handle, but good. The XR can always use a good hand."

"Doing what?" Ross asked easily. "Planting wheat?"

Sellew colored slightly, then the smile came back. "See you around, Parnell." He gave a slight wave with his right hand, wheeled his horse, and headed out in the direction of Hogtown.

The small ranchers stood there, watching him go, a mingled look of fear and hatred in their eyes. Gib Baudry, wiping his mouth with the back of his hand, opened the gate, then turned. He said, "I'll see you when you ain't standing a step above me, Parnell." He went through the gate and down the street, staying close to the fences, stopping now and then for a second, as if he were still sick.

Judge Iverson looked at the men grouped there on the steps in front of him—old friends and neighbors he had known for a long time. His voice was soft when he said, "Go on about your business, boys. Sellew is counting on trouble and you can bet he's got his crew here to back him up. Don't be fools and play into his hands."

The men turned sheepishly, saying nothing, and filed back down the walk. The judge went back into the house and sat down as if he were too tired to stand. He spread his hands and said, "That's how it is, Ross. Maybe you can see now why I couldn't take Agnes Fenton in my house. Trouble is like a boil here in the valley, and it keeps trying to come to a head. They've been six months now trying to fence in the north side of the XR. Wire gets cut faster than it gets strung."

The old man became thoughtful, and Ross, thinking back to the evenings he had spent in this very room, sensed the thoughts that were going through Judge Iverson's mind.

Ross spoke softly, as if he were thinking aloud, matching his thoughts with those of the judge. "You figure with the fence in she won't be able to say you boys along the river here are getting fat off her beef?"

The judge said, "There's always been two sides to a fence, Ross. Me and some of the others would have fenced long ago if we could have afforded it. We had a few bad years and it hasn't been good. Most of the boys are mortgaged over their heads and trouble now will break them."

"Who's fighting the fence, then?"

The judge spread his hands. "She says we are. Some of the boys here say she's doing it herself. They say she doesn't want a fence, that it's all a stall. It's not small time any more, Ross. She's losing cows a hundred at a time."

"What does her husband say?"

"All he cares about is fencing off land that's to be planted to wheat. He's even having trouble doing that."

"Why?" Ross asked softly.

"It costs money, Ross," the judge said. "A lot of money. Two different contractors have tried it here on the north side. They've both gone broke."

Ross got up slowly and stretched his muscles. The gun belt still lay there on the porch where he had dropped it, and he stepped out the open door and picked it up now, fumbling with it self-consciously, not knowing for sure what to do with it. He folded it finally, grinned sheepishly, held out the gun belt, and said, "Could I leave this here, Judge?"

"You know you can," the judge said. Then, "Necessity makes strange bedfellows, Ross. Don't have trouble with Baudry."

Ross laughed. "Not me. Gotta go look up the Hedleys and see that they get settled all right. Haven't squared up with the old man yet."

He mounted his horse and rode down Bridge Street and across the slough to the squalid meanness of Hogtown. A woman called his name joyfully. He turned in his saddle and saw her in a rocking chair on the porch of a cheap hotel. For a while he couldn't remember, and then he knew. She had been no more than sixteen a few years back, a kid who lived with her folks down the street a way and tried to keep her chin up when they hung her father. She seemed fifty now. She rocked her ponderous weight in her chair. The paint on her lips and cheeks stood out like gaudy patches. She said, "I've got my own place now, Ross. Heard tell you was back. Come over and see me." She cackled gleefully, and Ross rode on down the rutted street, feeling a crawling disgust.

There was the stench of old beer and half-rotted garbage, and the flies swarmed thickly on manure piles. He kept watching for the wagon and finally spotted it, pulled up behind a crumbling adobe shack that stood in the middle of a vacant weed-choked field without benefit of shade. He rode that way, dismounted, and went inside without being invited.

Sam Hedley was at a pine table in the dingy room, halfway through a plate of beans. He looked up, and some of the bean juice ran down the side of his mouth and dripped from his whiskers. He said, "Sit down, Ross. Been expecting you."

Ross said, "Where's the family, Sam?"

Sam Hedley grinned. "You mean Jean? Out seein' the town, I reckon."

"Look, Sam," Ross said earnestly. "I know you haven't made plans yet——" He paused, not sure of himself, not sure why he was concerned. "You know how towns are, Sam. Saboba's no different than any other. There's a right side of town and a wrong side of town."

Sam sucked the bean juice off his mustache. He said, "Agnes Fenton tells me there's a vacant house up the street here."

"You wouldn't want to settle your womenfolks over here," Ross said quickly.

Sam laid his spoon at the side of his plate and wiped his mouth with the palm of his hand. Looking up slowly, a half-challenge in his eyes, he said, "Mrs. Fenton strikes me as a lady. She lives here, don't she?"

It was like Sam to make an argument out of advice. Ross grinned and said, "I didn't mean it like that, Sam. I was thinking of you getting settled. Judge Iverson was saying there's school land that could be filed on."

Sam Hedley put both hands against the edge of the table and leaned back and looked up at Ross Parnell. He said, "I've heard of Judge Iverson, Parnell. I've seen how the XR works. I didn't come here to file on no quarter section of land and raise potatoes and I didn't come here to get run off, neither. There's free grass hereabouts and I aim to have myself some of it. That's why I come here, Ross. I got it in me to grow as big as the XR and maybe that's what I aim to do. A man don't grow that big takin' charity from the likes of Judge Iverson. You brought us here and now your job's done. Don't hang around trying to pass out advice to a man twice your age. So long, Parnell."

A hard knot of anger had been forming in Ross's middle. The skin on his face felt tight, and he said, "There's a little matter of two hundred dollars first, Sam."

Sam Hedley, still leaning back, grinned crookedly. He said, "There is. And soon's I get lined out and sell some beef I aim to pay you that two hundred dollars."

Ross felt the muscles tighten along his forearms and his hands opened and closed without any control on his part. A voice from the dimness of the back room said, "You heard him, Parnell. Get goin'. We'll pay you your two hundred dollars when we get it." Young Bret came out of the back room and stood by his father's chair. He had a six-shooter in his hand, not pointed at Ross, not pointed at anything, just laying in his hands, as if perhaps he had been cleaning it.

For a long time Ross watched them, then he grinned and shook his head. "I was wrong," he said. "You'll fit well here in Hogtown." He went back outside and mounted, and rode down the main street with its bagnios and cheap saloons.

Near the edge of town he saw Maw Hedley and Agnes Fenton and Jean. Maw was beaming and smiling in that vacant way of hers, looking at things that Agnes Fenton pointed out, seeing only what she wanted to see. She might as well have been on the main street of Kansas City.

Jean's face was drawn and white, her eyes wide. A man whistled, and Ross heard Agnes say, "Don't pay no mind to him, dearie. The boys act kinda rough but they're jest as good as gold, every one of them. You'll see when you meet some of them."

Jean saw Ross, and she called and started across the street toward him. Ross swallowed hard against a lump that had come to his throat, touched his spurs to his horse's flanks, and rode on. He heard Jean call his name once, and a quick swell of feeling pressed up in his chest, dried his mouth. He started to rein in his horse and then he thought, "The hell with it. No woman's going to make a fool of me a second time!" He rode on, straight down the street. It seemed he could feel the hurt surprise of Jean Hedley pressing against his back. He gigged the horse into a trot, heading back for the main section of Saboba.

Now, for the first time, a cold anger started growing toward Sam Hedley and Bret, and gradually it spread to include Jean, but when it did there was a certain pain mixed with the anger. This was no quick decision, this refusing to pay him his two hundred dollars. It had been planned since the beginning of the trip, back there in Kansas. He remembered how closely knit as a family the Hedleys were, remembered the nights when he had felt as lonely as the space and the stars, shut out from this very closeness. Then, if it had been planned, Jean must have known. He swung down in front of a stable, led his horse inside. To the stableman's inquiry as to how long he planned on leaving the horse Ross snapped, "How in hell should I know?" He went back on the street, pulling his hat down over his eyes.

It was his own damned fault, he told himself. He had come back to Saboba for one purpose—to settle once and for all with Trip Levitt. At the same time he wanted to prove he had conquered his feeling for Lenore. Failed on both scores, he reminded himself, and he kicked at a tin can that was lying in the dust.

As for the Hedleys, they had been a nonentity when he started; they were that now. In the way a man has when making excuses for himself Ross turned his blame on something tangible: Jean Hedley. She had been the bait; she had been the one who had asked him to take meals with them. Until then he had played it alone. The hell with them, he told himself promptly. He was through with them now, and two hundred dollars was cheap enough for the lesson. He came to a saloon, half-saw the sign, BEN FRANSEN, and went inside.

It was more than a year since Ross Parnell had had more than two drinks at one time, but now the sourness of whisky and beer that hung in the still air of the deserted room tickled his senses and touched his palate and his stomach. He hadn't eaten since breakfast and he was hungry. Part of his rebellion turned against his own decisions and he went up to the bar and slapped his palm for a drink. The one bartender on duty was slow in responding. Ross said, "Sleep later, friend. Whisky."

The drink burned as he gulped it down in one throw; it lay hot and tempting in the pit of his stomach. He had another quick one, then, catching sight of himself in the mirror, he felt a twinge of guilt. He was being childish, a spoiled brat who hadn't been able to have his own way. He looked around the room, trying to spot someone he knew.

It was a big saloon, though not ornate. The bar ran the complete length of the room, and the back bar and mirrors were the only showy things in the place. There were gambling layouts set more or less to themselves at the far end of the room, and there was a small stage, coy behind coping saw-scrolls and a dusty plum-colored velvet curtain. The three dice tables were covered with a green cloth; the faro layout was deserted. A string of slot machines beckoned half-heartedly with their single arms; a Mexican croupier dozed on a high stool near the roulette wheel. The dealer moved now and then to brush at a fly that seemed eternally near his nose. Ross paid for his drinks with a twenty-dollar gold-piece, the only money he had. The bartender slid back nineteen dollars and fifty cents.

Five of it Ross put in a wallet in his back pocket. It would pay for the stabling of the horse. The rest he left lying on the bar. The bartender said, "Another drink, stranger?"

"If I want it, I'll pour it," Ross said.

Once he thought of riding back to Hogtown and having it out with the Hedleys; Jean kept getting in his way. Once he thought of going over to the judge's, getting his gun, and riding. He couldn't bring himself to do it; his actions weren't something he wanted Judge Iverson to see. He ground out a cigarette in an ash tray, scooped up his money, and walked over to the roulette wheel. The Mexican cut off a half-finished snore, adjusted his eyeshade. Ross said, "Ten dollars on the double-O."

The Mexican grinned. He said, "Whole peeg or nothing, no?" Ross didn't answer.

The Mexican's deft fingers spun the wheel. The ball clicked and danced, hopped crazily, caught, and spun in an indistinguishable blur of red and black. The wheel slowed, and Ross felt a surge of excitement that he tried to conceal. The Mexican pushed back his eyeshade and remarked, "The wheel must have been talking to you, señor. A quick way to make two hundred dollars."

The unadulterated thrill it gave him, combined with the amount, sent a reckless twinge of pleasure charging through Ross's veins. Gambling was another thing he had quit, but here he had played a long shot, and he had won. He looked at the pile of chips, and without even planning to say it he said, "Two hundred on the same."

The Mexican was wide awake now. He looked at Ross closely, shrugged his shoulders, spun the wheel. The bartender moved down toward the end of the bar; he was leaning on his elbows, as if it didn't matter much; he had caught the same trickle of excitement that was in Ross. The ball kept dancing and bouncing as if it would leave the race. Ross's breathing became shallow in his lungs. There was a long, flat silence. The Mexican said, "That is seven thousand dollars, señor. In the daytime we do not keep so much at the wheel. I will go to the safe for the money."

Ross didn't answer. His mouth was dry. He pushed his tongue against the inside of his lips and called for the bottle. "One for yourself and one for the dealer," he said. "I don't like to drink alone."

7

WHEN TUCK BRANT had ridiculed him in front of half of Saboba, Ross Parnell had been young. He had started gambling and drinking to prove that he was as tough and as hard as the next one—a child's way of fighting his own emotions.

By his actions he had lost few friends that mattered; he had found one that counted: Judge Iverson. For the judge had a way of looking inside a man and seeing the things that drove him to actions that were outside his basic character. He had spoken to Ross about it, not constantly, in a nagging way, but once. He had said only, "It's an old saw, Ross: A man is known by the company he keeps. Vance Levitt and some of the others haven't got too sweet a reputation."

But it had taken a shock like that night in Jim East's

saloon to bring Ross to his senses. Until that night it had never entered his mind that he might someday kill a man, and when it was over, and he was in the single cell of Saboba's jail, he was amazed to find out how much of a child he actually was.

It was self-defense, the jury decided. It was a fair fight. Yet the feeling was still there, unerased by a jury's verdict; he had killed a man, and it wasn't a pretty thing to contemplate.

He had thought little of Trip Levitt then. Vaguely he knew there was an older brother; rumor had it that Trip Levitt was serving a stretch in prison for a stage robbery.

They buried Vance Levitt in boot hill and Hogtown came to the funeral. The town was quiet, and Ross Parnell was alone, left to live out his life with himself. Lenore Brant had written him a letter, making it sound as if he were a knight who had worn her handkerchief into a joust. It sickened him.

So he left Saboba, and the sharp tongue of gossip built a story around his doings. Then, one night, far in the south of Texas, he heard a small man whisper and point with his thumb and say, "He killed a man over a woman in Saboba. They say he's afraid to go back." It was a thing that would warp a man, and though Ross Parnell grew, he came to realize finally that his emotions had not grown to a stature that would match his body. Emotion had been arrested and stopped that night in Saboba.

Sometimes at night there was little sleep, and he thought of Lenore Brant, and how it had happened because of her. And he wondered if he had loved her, if he still loved her, and in time he knew that he would have to go back and wipe out the shadows before he could become whole again.

There was no drinking after that, and he threw away the cards that he packed in his saddlebag. But he was a man with the blood of the frontier in his veins—the same blood that had sent lonely, buckskin-clad figures wandering into an unknown land to live with the Indians and search for the beaver pelt. His blood had been at the Alamo and again with the filibusters who pushed south toward Sonora. It was blood that could be stirred by a vision of trackless space and the dust of a trail herd; by the blaze of a gun. It was blood that would not lie cool and placid when a roulette wheel bounced its fickle sphere into two straight double-O's.

He felt it charging through him now, and he knew that his cheeks were flushed with it, and his hands, had he not fought against it, would have been unsteady. The bartender had his drink and he said, "That's only the third time I ever seen that happen, mister."

"To Lady Luck," said Ross Parnell.

He had no illusions as to why the Mexican dealer had gone to the safe to get his winnings. When a man's luck hit like his had it was time to inform the big boss. Ross said, "Ben Fransen run this place?"

"He does that," the bartender said.

Ross decided he would be seeing Ben Fransen. But he didn't, right then. The Mexican came back and counted out the seven thousand dollars, and when he had pushed the last of it across the table, he said only, "You sure peek a lucky one that time, señor." He reached over then, and gave the wheel a spin, letting the little ball make its siren music against the stops.

Ross shook his head. "I'll let it cool a bit. I like to change off, anyway. How long before the dice tables open up?"

"Not until seven o'clock," said the Mexican, giving the wheel another twirl. "Quite a while weeth not much to do."

"I'm not going any place," Ross said.

He knew the ways of a roulette wheel, and realized that it was the easiest gadget in the house to fix. With seven thousand dollars of Ben Fransen's money it was only reasonable to suppose that they had picked him to have too many drinks and make one rash bet. At the same time, walking out with that much money was a poor way to make friends with a gambler. He peeled off twenty dollars, handed it to the Mexican, and said, "We'll give it a try later."

He had another drink, and, except for a dull uneasiness that was always with him, forgot the Hedleys and, in a way, Trip Levitt. The feel of money started itching in his soul like a gnawing disease, and he had a rosy-flushed vision of breaking this place and of walking out with his pockets bulging. A few years back, he would have finished that dream with a milk-white horse and a silver-mounted saddle—a horse that fretted and pawed and curvetted in front of Lenore Brant. It was hell how much of the child remained in a grown man.

Two men he didn't know came in; wheat farmers, maybe. They could have been. And a while later a lone XR puncher drifted by. Ross bought him a drink and had one himself. The four men made up a poker game —a friendly thing with low stakes. After losing a few pots, a good one came along, and Ross Parnell drew two cards to fill a flush. He knew, then, his god was riding his shoulders tonight, and he'd be a fool to quit.

The farmers left, breaking off the game. Ross put a silver dollar into one of the slot machines. Three plums showed up, giving him sixteen dollars back.

He bought a round of drinks after that, and had to dig into his pocket for an extra dollar. He hadn't noticed that the evening crowd was starting to come in. A familiar voice said, "Thanks, Parnell." He shifted his weight slightly, and saw Tony Sellew standing there, with that same smile on his face, and a jigger of whisky in his hand.

Sellew said, "Hear your luck's been running good."

Ross said, "News travels fast."

"It does," Sellew admitted. "Gonna shoot some craps? I'd like to ride it with you."

Ross shrugged. "Why not?"

He was calmly relaxed and a long way from drunk and he found that it was easy now to laugh at his experience with the Hedleys. Money could do that to him. It became difficult only when he let his thoughts dwell too long on Jean. He wondered why that was. He wasn't in love with the girl, he knew, because there was none of that surging, crazy, tumultuous drive that had been in him when he had loved Lenore Brant. This was only a steady uneasiness that pricked him and bothered him when he thought of her. And yet the disturbing thought touched him once that he could always remember the exact color of Jean Hedley's eyes; he could not, for the life of him, remember Lenore's, except that there was a certain calculating hardness there.

He threw snake eyes on the first toss of the cubes, and he laughed, and said, "That's a good sign."

Tony Sellew, backing Ross to make his point, said, "Good sign or not, I'll never get rich that way."

The fourth time he took the dice, they felt right in his hand. He could have told it even before they bounced off the backstop and came to rest there in the middle of the green table. Somebody said, "As big and fat a seven as I ever looked at."

Another said, "Natural Davis, so help me."

It started then. He didn't know how much. A man was crazy to stop and count when a thing like this happened to him. His face was flushed and he was giddy with excitement. There was none of the cold, calculating gambler about him; he was a kid with ten dollars at a circus.

"Ten's the point," he said. "How you want it, boys?"

A man who had backed him with dollar bets, refusing to let them ride, said gleefully, "Let's see it with two fives."

Ross blew on the dice, tossed them out. Two beautiful fives winked back at him from the green.

They changed housemen, not once, but four times. They went once to the safe and brought out more money. The bar was deserted. They stood ten deep around the dice table, and now and then Ross said, "A drink for the crowd."

And then, as suddenly as it had come to him, he knew it had turned. He lost the dice three times in a row. He grinned and said, "Get off my back, boys. The little lady with the silver spurs has taken a walk."

Sellew said, "It's good enough for me, boy. Quit snapping your fingers and have a drink. You've already worn 'em down to the first knuckle."

"I'm quitting for a while," Ross said to the housemen. "Cash 'em in and we'll try it later."

They sat down at a table, he and Tony Sellew, and Ross said, "Shall we make up a poker game?"

Sellew laughed good-naturedly. "Not with you we don't," he said. "You've got one of those nights a man dreams about."

Even with the luck he had had, he couldn't believe it when they paid him off. He had won ten thousand dollars. Sellew shook his head. "Another hour of that and you'd own the place."

"Another round for the house," Ross said smugly.

A girl came over to their table, a small, fragile, pretty little thing with too much paint. She put her arm around Tony Sellew's neck, and with her left hand rumpled his hair. She smiled, a practiced smile, and somehow swayed her body against Tony. "Introduce me to Mr. Lucky," she said.

"Ross Parnell—Queenie." Sellew said it in a half-irritated manner. Then, "Go sing my song, baby."

The girl said, "How about a little drink? It ought to be champagne."

"Sing my song," said Sellew.

Queenie stood there, her body swaying away from Tony Sellew. She put her hand on her left hip, twisted slightly, and, reaching out, pressed her finger against the tip of Ross Parnell's nose. "You're handsome too," she said.

Sellew told her, "I said, sing my song."

"Sure, Tony."

She walked over to the piano in the corner, a swaying, undulating walk. The piano player laid his cigar on the already-scarred top, took a quick gulp out of his mug of beer, and started beating the keys. The tune drifted off into a slow, mournful cadence that Queenie matched with her body. She started to sing, a high, plaintive wail of a voice that dripped with emotion:

> *"Take back the ring you gave me,*
> *Take it back, Jack, I pray.*
> *Wearing it would deprave me*
> *More than I am today.*
> *To make me your wife would wrong you,*
> *Grief to your heart would bring,*
> *So please take it back,*
> *I beg of you, Jack!*
> *Take back the en-gage-a-ment ring!"*

A long-drawn-out, tear-heavy last line. Tony Sellew had another drink.

The girl came back to the table and this time she took a chair next to Ross Parnell. "How about that drink now, Mr. Lucky?"

"Pretty song, beautiful," Ross said. "Name it."

"I said champagne."

"You'll get it."

Queenie looked at him for a second, then leaned forward quickly, put her arms around his neck, and kissed him hard on the lips. She withdrew her mouth slowly and in a whisper said, "You're lucky—and handsome—and you're generous. What more could any woman want?"

There was a slight spot of color in Tony Sellew's cheeks. He said, "And you're damn free with your kisses, Queenie."

"Forget it," Ross said.

"Sure," Sellew said, the dark flush apparent now. "I forgot for a minute, a man lucky at gambling is seldom lucky in love."

There seemed to be a dangling implication in the statement. Ross met the XR ramrod's eyes, then he laughed. "To hell with it," he said.

He left a fifty-dollar bill on the table, got up, and pushed his way through the crowd. A portly man with curly iron-gray hair and mustaches with waxed tips got in his way. The man wore a well-fitted vest with stamped horseshoes, and an expensively tailored coat. He said, "I like to see a man lucky in my place. It draws trade."

"A way of saying you're Ben Fransen?" asked Ross.

"One way." Fransen nodded his head shortly. "Another is seeing a man get a good piece of land, if that's what he's after. Or running a survey to find land that's claimed by the wrong folks." Fransen laughed. "There's some here say I'm a good man to know."

Ross said, "Nothing like admitting it."

"Good to see you quitting," said Fransen. "A man gets a streak of luck like that, he can only push it so far."

"You figure mine's gone, then?"

Fransen shrugged his shoulders. "Just friendly advice. In this business sometimes you win, sometimes you lose. I like to see a new man get the right start in this town, that's all."

"I'm not new," Ross said. "I was raised here. Maybe that makes your advice no good. Cut cards for a drink?"

Fransen laughed. "The man trusts me."

"Why not?" Ross said. "I don't know you."

"Deck, Joe." The bartender tossed a new deck of cards to his boss. Fransen broke the seal, shuffled them deftly, and passed them across to Ross. Ross shuffled them twice and pushed them back.

"You brought the new folks in today, didn't you?" Fransen asked. "What's the name? Hedley? Too bad about Loop Fenton. Feel sorry for his wife. Hedley. Yeah, believe that's it."

"Hedley," Ross said.

"The kid was in talking to me. Seems like a smart boy."

Ross's hand hesitated a moment over the deck. He looked at Ben Fransen, trying to find something in the man's eyes. He saw nothing. He cut and turned over a three. Fransen grinned, and said, "See what I told you?" He turned the next card. It was the deuce of spades. "I'll be damned," he said.

"Maybe it's because I was raised here," said Ross. "I'll have rye."

"My private bottle, Joe," Ben Fransen ordered. "Cigar, Parnell?"

"You know my name, then," said Ross, accepting the cigar.

"A man's name is a handy tool," Ben Fransen remarked, offering a light. "I make it my business to know names."

"Regards," Ross said, and held up his glass.

There was a loud, piercing squeal. Over at the table Tony Sellew threw back his head and laughed. The girl, Queenie, was on her feet, her eyes blazing. She lashed out and slapped Sellew hard, across the cheek. Tony got up, lurching slightly, his face darkly red. He grabbed the girl, turned her across his knee, and spanked her hard. Men roared with laughter. Fransen, shaking his head, said, "Sellew and his damn women. They can't leave him alone and they always get the worst of it."

Ross was paying little attention to either the spanking

or to Ben Fransen's words. In the struggle Tony Sellew's coat had opened and pushed back, and against the whiteness of his shirt Ross saw the unmistakable blackness of a shoulder-holstered gun. Tony got to his feet quickly, took the girl's face in both his hands, and kissed her on the lips, holding her that way for minutes. Men whistled and stamped their feet. The girl beat ineffective fists against Tony Sellew's back and gradually her arms relaxed at her sides and then went up and encircled Tony's neck. Tony pushed her away and said, "Go sing my song, sweetheart."

"I sang it once."

"Go sing my song."

The piano started its dirge-like, metallic rattle. The girl, her face flushed with color, her eyes bright, clasped her hands and started to sing.

> *"Take back the ring you gave me,*
> *Take it back, Jack, I pray——"*

And, suddenly, it was not the dancehall girl who was standing there singing. It was Lenore Brant Warrington that Ross Parnell saw, and a hot, knifing cut that was almost jealousy laced through him. He remembered nights a long time back, and he heard his own voice coming back to him, *"What do you want a man to do? Slap you down and drag you off?"*

"Did you say something?" Ben Fransen asked.

"No. Should I have?"

Fransen laughed. "Come back to earth," he said. "That's Sellew's property. I asked you if you would be interested in putting that luck of yours in a private game."

The liquor had taken hold in Ross's stomach. It rolled around, warm and good, unencumbered by the food he had not yet eaten. It gave him a quick recklessness. He looked at Tony Sellew, tilted back in his chair, thumbs hooked in his belt. He thought of the gun that was there under the man's coat and he thought of Lenore and of the sneer that had been on Herbert Warrington's face when he had introduced Ross to Tony Sellew. And he thought of Sam Hedley and Bret, and, most of all, he thought of Jean. But somehow he didn't want to think of her while he was standing here looking over Tony Sellew's head, watching Queenie sing.

He tried to shrug off a bit of rebellion that had reached out and touched him time and again in these past few years, and the corners of his mouth pulled down some. For a few minutes this afternoon with old Maria, there at Judge Iverson's house, he had been Ross Parnell, the young puncher who rode the open range with the wind in his face and the sun in his eyes—a puncher with dreams bigger than the land; a puncher in love with a girl who had cattle in her blood and land in her heart and the power in her eyes to burn a man's soul to hell.

Now it was gone, and he was a saddle tramp who had killed a man over a woman. He turned and looked straight into the eyes of Ben Fransen; he said, "Sure, I'll play you some poker. Why not?"

Ben Fransen smiled, and nodded his head toward the stairway that led up to the rooms on the second floor. As they started across the room together, a red-lipped and tight-waisted girl saw them, and pushed her way through the crowd. She smiled invitingly at Ross: "Hi, Lucky. Did you want me, Ben?"

Ben Fransen shook his head. "This is poker." The girl seemed disappointed.

They went up the stairs together, Ben Fransen and Ross Parnell. They entered a well-furnished room near the head of the stairs; Fransen nudged the door closed behind him. He went to a closet, brought out a bottle and glasses, and set them on the small, round, green-topped table. "Sit down, Parnell," he invited. "I like to relax like this now and then."

From downstairs the voice of the girl floated up, muffled by the flooring:

> *"Take back the ring you gave me,*
> *Take it back, Jack, I pray——"*

8

BEN FRANSEN, Ross soon found, was a man full of surprises. Ross had played an amazing streak of luck at Fransen's expense. He had close to ten thousand dollars in his pocket, and when he came upstairs to play a two-handed game of cards he had fully expected Fransen to try to take that ten thousand. He entered the game of his own free will because he felt it was one of those nights. His luck was hot and unbeatable, and it would stay that way. Fransen sat there savoring his drink like a man used to good liquor. He said, "Nickel a chip and a two-bit limit, shall we?"

Ross translated that into dollars and was still somewhat surprised that the man would suggest a limit on this particular game. Fransen fished some nickels and dimes and quarters out of his vest pocket and laid the coins on the table. Seeing Ross's look of surprise, he said, "I mean it. I told you I like to relax like this sometimes. When I play cards, I play for fun. I don't like to have to worry about money."

Ross shook his head and grinned. There was something almost likable about the big, gray-haired man, but at the same time there was a frostiness in his eyes that held a man at arm's length. Ross said, "You caught me off guard. I figured you'd play for blood."

"Not with cards," Fransen said, and let the remark go unexplained.

The apartment was well furnished, in good taste. There was a silken bell rope in one corner of the room; when they had played a few hands without talking much, Fransen signaled, and one of the bartenders came up from downstairs. "Bring us a couple of good steaks," said Fransen. "How are things going?"

"Word has spread about this fellow's luck. The wheel is getting a hell of a play."

"Tell Jack to use his own judgment," said Fransen. When the bartender had left, he ruffled the cards and remarked, "It doesn't hurt to let them win once in a while. They're always sucker enough to come back."

"Was the wheel fixed for me to win?" Ross asked.

The question didn't make the slightest ruffle in Fransen's composure. "Funny part of it is," he said, "it wasn't. The wheel was perfectly straight when you played it. Would it have bothered you to find out it was set?"

"Why should it?" Ross shrugged. "I've played crooked wheels before."

"That's what I figured," Fransen said.

The steaks came up, thick and juicy, done exactly right. The tantalizing smell of them reminded Ross that he hadn't eaten since breakfast and he fell to hungrily, cleaning his plate. Sipping his black coffee, well laced with good brandy, he drew deeply on the expensive cigar Fransen had provided and said, "You have things nice here."

"I do," said Fransen, with no touch of bragging. "I'll have them better. You made any plans?"

"None."

"I might be able to use a man with luck like yours."

"I'll listen."

Fransen's shrewd blue eyes watched Ross carefully, as if they could pick every reaction, every emotion off Ross's

face; as if they could look inside a man's skull and decipher the meaning of the workings there. He said, "I
made a mistake and located a couple of farmers between
the Catclaw and the escarpment out there at the east end
of the XR range. I been hoping they'd get discouraged
and go back to Kansas."

Fransen's probing eyes never wavered, but Ross gave
the man nothing to see. He said, "If these farmers did get
discouraged and decided to leave, maybe you'd make a
mistake and sell that land again. That it?"

"Or maybe I'd just be doing somebody a favor," Fransen said.

"You got enough of that kind of work to keep a man
busy?" Ross asked.

"That's my business," Fransen said.

Ross had a completely new appraisal of the man now.
Ben Fransen was shrewd, cold as ice, without an ounce
of fear or conscience in him. He was the kind of man,
Ross saw, who would cover his tracks well; the kind of
man who would hire his killing done. It struck him as
odd that Fransen would take him even this far into his
confidence, considering the fact that Fransen didn't know
him. And then a cold prickle of apprehension ran up
Ross's spine. He realized suddenly that it was Fransen's
way of showing him that no man could buck him. If Ross
were to prove troublesome, he might be found at the
bottom of a coulee. There was only one way to talk to a
man like that. Ross said, "I'm not ready to go to work
yet."

To all outward appearances Fransen was completely
unconcerned. He said, "That's all right. I just wanted you
to know how I stand around here. I told you once some
people say I'm a good man to know."

"I'll remember it," said Ross.

There was the heavy tread of boots out in the hall, then
a sharp rap on the door. As unconcerned as if he had been

getting a toothpick or a match, Fransen pulled open the drawer in a small stand and took out a loaded six-shooter. He stuffed it in the waistband of his trousers and pulled his coat closed, hiding the weapon. After that he walked to the door and opened it. Gib Baudry came in.

Catching the look that shot between Baudry and Ross, Fransen said, "You two know each other?"

Baudry's left eye was swollen shut, and his lips were split wickedly. Ross said, "Yeah. We know each other."

"You look like you got kicked by a horse, Baudry," said Fransen.

Baudry stood there, big, coarse-featured, sullen, and stupid. He was plainly caught off guard, seeing Ross here, and he didn't know what to say. Fransen put the words in the big man's mouth. He said, "I'll have to think it over, Gib. Anyway, it's too late at night to talk business. See me tomorrow morning and I'll let you know one way or the other, for sure."

Gib Baudry was a poor actor. He blinked stupidly a few times, gradually caught on, and seemed to be pleased that he had. Without ever having uttered a single word he turned and went out into the hall, slamming the door behind him.

Fransen looked steadily at Ross Parnell, and Ross remembered the gun the man had stuffed in his waistband. There was a half-smile on Fransen's lips. He said, "Gib wanted to borrow some money from me. That's what he came to see me about."

Ross shrugged his shoulders. "It's no affair of mine," he said.

Fransen nodded slowly, the smile still on his lips. "That's exactly right, Parnell."

Then suddenly he was the jovial, friendly land locator and saloon owner. He slapped Ross on the back affectionately, and said, "Been nice knowing you. I won't forget the money you won. Watch your bets next time, or I'll take it away from you."

It was jesting, friendly banter, yet the statement seemed to be double-edged, and one of those edges was viciously sharp, saw-toothed and dangerous. Ross said, "What the hell, you're four bits to the good in this game."

"And I had to feed you a dollar steak to win that," said Fransen.

They sounded like friends saying good night after a harmless evening, and yet neither man was underestimating the other. Fransen had come out openly and told Ross that if he planned to stay in Saboba he had best get on the band wagon. Ross thought of young Bret Hedley, hot-tempered, impressionable, and he remembered that Fransen had said the kid had been to see him. He remembered, too, that Judge Iverson had been worried about Fransen seeing the Hedleys. Gib Baudry hadn't come here at this hour about borrowing money.

Ross said good night, and went out in the hall and downstairs. It was after two o'clock in the morning, and the place was crowded to overflowing. He noticed that Tony Sellew was still at the same table, his arm around Queenie, the girl who had sung the song for him.

The big room was noisy and close, choking with cigarette smoke and whisky fumes. He saw Sellew glance his way; he couldn't tell whether the XR foreman had seen him or not. He pushed open the door and went outside into the cool night air and the sweetness of new spring and young grass. He stood there on the porched-over sidewalk, making a cigarette.

Two men walked down the dark side of the street. One snapped a cigarette off his thumbnail; it made a tiny comet in the night. Farther up the line, across the slough, Hogtown was having a time for itself. Ross thought of the girl on the porch of the hotel; he thought of Jean Hedley.

The tension of the gambling was running out of him and a slight chill shook his frame although the night was not cold. There to the south, along the dark rim of the Sasinaw, he could make out the shapes of the warehouses and the deserted lumberyard. Beyond that, he knew, was the endless plain, the land of the XR, stretching south through uninhabited and unclaimed miles of grass and wicked canyon slashes to the Mexican border. But it wasn't, he realized suddenly, uninhabited and unclaimed now.

The fence stood across the land four strands high; it was like an ending in a land that had been endless. Devil rope, laying its barbed demarcation between cattle and wheat, but here on this north line there was no fence, and men still fought and suspected each other. Men still died.

Above the thin fan of the town glare the stars looked down, wise and unchanged. And it occurred to Ross that with the coming of this fence, Saboba had made itself even more of a battleground.

If the XR had stopped itself from southern expansion (and it had done that by Herbert Warrington's own design), then it would start expanding north, crossing the multi-owned loops of the Sasinaw, into the small ranches of Gib Baudry and old Ed Tozier; into the land of Judge Iverson and into the town of Saboba itself. He could see how the small ranchers might decide the XR didn't want this north fence. He thought of Ben Fransen, cold, unruffled, more sure of himself than any man Ross had ever met, and he wondered what part Fransen would play in this new scheme of things.

He suddenly became conscious of the money he was packing, and started up the street toward the stable where he had left his horse, then crossed over and headed down toward Judge Iverson's, where he knew Maria would have a bed for him. He had gone less than two blocks when he knew he was being followed.

The money in his pocket became a heavy weight that pulled against him; the absence of his gun belt was a pressing vacancy around his middle. A breeze moved, and he felt the cool touch of evaporated perspiration on his forehead. He quickened his step some, and heard the footsteps behind him match his own. He stopped flat, then, and the voice of Trip Levitt said, "All right, Parnell. There's no woman's skirt to hide behind this time. Turn around and get it in the guts."

The flesh crawled on Ross's spine, and each hair of his head seemed to become an individual hair, making itself conspicuous by its presence in his scalp. He turned slowly, keeping his hands away from his side. Trip Levitt was standing there, hulking and big, his lips pulled back from his teeth. He wore no gun belt but his right hand was in the pocket of his denim jumper, and even in the darkness Ross could see the outline where Trip's hand gripped a gun. Rather than accenting the wave of cold panic he had felt, the sight of the gun seemed to calm Ross. He said softly, "I haven't got a gun, Trip. Let me get one and we'll have it out."

"My kid brother might as well not had a gun the night you shot him," Trip Levitt said. "He's just as dead." He sucked air through his teeth, as if testing the flavor of the moment. He said, "It's taken a long time, Parnell." Trip's hand lifted from his pocket and the gun was there, black, hard. His thumb hooked back the hammer.

"It was a fair fight, Trip. You weren't there to see it, and maybe you didn't hear it straight."

"I like to hear you whinin' like that."

Trip took two steps forward, slow, deliberate steps, as if he knew that each fall of his foot was jarring through Ross's body. He raised the gun on a line with Ross's middle. A voice, low, vibrant, without tension, said, "Drop it, Trip!"

Trip Levitt seemed to freeze. It took only the tightening of his finger against the trigger and Ross Parnell would be dead. And still he hesitated, and in that eternity of hesitation the same voice said, "God damn you, Trip, drop it!"

Trip Levitt's hand opened, and the gun fell to the sidewalk there by his feet. There was a soft, noiseless movement and then Ben Fransen was standing there, a six-shooter pressed against Trip Levitt's back. His voice was soft and deadly and he said, "Get the hell out of town, Trip. A long ways out of town." He thrust with the gun, and Trip Levitt hurried into the night as if propelled by the impact of Fransen's words. Fransen thrust the gun back into the waistband of his trousers and he pulled his coat forward and buttoned it.

The after-drive of emotion swept through Ross Parnell's body now. He knew he was sweating profusely and there was a weakness in his knees, a certain unsteadiness in his voice. He tried to cover it by expelling his breath and saying, "Thanks, Fransen—a close squeak. Maybe you *are* a good man to know."

"I don't mix in personal quarrels, Parnell," Fransen said flatly. "I'm not obliged to you for getting me in this one."

Ross fumbled with an answer, taken off guard by the man's tone of voice. Finally he said, "I'll make it my job to see Trip Levitt don't bother you none."

"You owe me no favor, Parnell," said Ben Fransen. "I was protecting myself. If you had been killed tonight they would have said it was because you won too much of my money. Folks are looking for things like that to say. If you had been killed tonight it would have been bad for business. If you want to save that money, I have a bank. If you want to play it, come in any time. Good night, Parnell." He turned and disappeared as abruptly as he had come, and Ross felt at that second more fear of Ben Fransen than he had felt toward Trip Levitt.

He hurried on toward Judge Iverson's then, testing each shadow before entering it, keeping wide of alleys and spaces between buildings. The light in Iverson's house was warm and inviting. He went around to the back door, hoping he could let himself in without disturbing Maria or the judge. He found the judge sitting at a table in the kitchen. The old man was surrounded with papers and ledgers. With his shirt collar open and his sleeves rolled, he looked even older than he had this afternoon. He smiled when he saw Ross, and said, "I was worried."

"I'm sorry as hell, Judge," Ross said sincerely. "I told you there'd be no trouble." He'd wait until morning to tell the judge of his gambling; he'd wait a long time before mentioning Trip Levitt.

"The town has changed some, eh, Ross?"

"A bit," Ross admitted. Then, "Who's this Ben Fransen, Judge?"

The judge studied his hands, spread them, and shrugged his thin shoulders. He looked like a man whipped by an unknown. He said, "That's a fair question, Ross. A man's not long in Saboba nowadays until he asks that."

9

THE RAILROAD had given Ben Fransen to Saboba, Judge Iverson said. The thought of steel rails fingering across the high plains had touched off excitement with a magic fire. Saboba had become drunk with its importance, and the town had burst into full-bloom life. The small ranchers who had dozed there north of the Sasinaw had begun to spend money for repairs long needed, and had talked of fabulous futures.

Old Dan Murdock, who owned the most westerly ranch, had come riding into Saboba for the first time in ten years. He had claimed the whole plains country had gone crazy and would come to no good, but he had bought a new blue shirt and mentioned in an offhand way that he reckoned the first damn thing a man knew there'd be lumber available.

And Diego Palomar of Rancho Los Lobos, situated between Dan Murdock and Ed Tozier, had felt the intoxication of it. It was like the first sip of the wine Diego kept in his cellar. Don he had been in the old days, and now don he was again as the two white horses had pulled the phaeton into Saboba. At Don Diego's side had been his wife, waxlike, transparent. It seemed that if one would touch her she would disintegrate. She had smiled, and Don Diego had doffed his low-crowned hat. He was proud.

Ed Tozier, as always, had had a few pessimistic observations to make. "The rails ain't here yet," he had whined, "don't never forget that. And how do you know when she does get here you're all gonna make the money you say you are? Times have been tough, don't never forget that, and they can be tougher. The railroad ain't in business fer your and my health, and don't you never forget that, neither."

Judge Iverson sighed as he remembered those first golden days. Ross Parnell, seeing the dreams in the eyes of his old friend, said, "You must have had quite a time for yourself."

"Saboba, Queen of the Plains." The judge laughed at himself. "How long ago was it I started booming Saboba, Ross?" he mused. "This looked like the real thing."

It was then that Gib Baudry and Loop Fenton, realizing the possible change in things, had decided they had had enough of living off strays from the XR. Loop hadn't located land yet, but there was land to be had, and Baudry already had a pretty nice spread there to the east of town.

Meetings and formal declarations were the order of the day, and at one of these meetings Judge Iverson, presiding, spoke solemnly to his neighbors. Good men, those neighbors; good men if they were guided. Crotchety old Dan Murdock; dapper Don Diego Palomar, a piece of the past; complaining and disgruntled Ed Tozier. Cattlemen, these three, and men who had made their way honestly. Joined with them that night was a fawning and anxious-to-please Gib Baudry and a contrite Loop Fenton. They formed a loosely drawn association, those six, and under Judge Iverson's directions they made simple rules to live as peaceful men in harmony with their giant neighbor to the south. Tuck Brant, although he had been invited, did not attend the meeting.

Saboba by now was a broiling melting pot of speculators and land-hungry cattlemen. "We six will have to pull together," the judge told them. "We are the backbone, and the stability of our new order depends on our keeping intact, keeping our place as cattlemen. New men will build the farms; the big operation—the XR—is already here. I've been preaching for twenty years that there's room in this country for places like ours and Tuck Brant's and plenty left over for those who want to farm it. You are watching the birth of an empire, boys."

Saboba—the XR—the breaks of the Sasinaw, and the rich land. It pyramided like a jewel-decked Christmas tree, and like a shining star at the very apex was the marriage of Lenore Brant and Herbert Warrington. There was no man here who didn't remember the dazzling spectacle of that occasion. There was no woman who didn't think of it some time, and pose the mute question of her kind: "Would I rather be rich, or poor and happy?"

And into this dazzle came Ben Fransen, and before he was two days settled in town he had made his presence felt. For one thing, he was a representative of the railroad, and at that time any man connected with the railroad was God. They feted Ben Fransen, and they accepted him, and they liked the polish he brought to the town that was to be the Jewel of the Plains.

He was no ordinary man, this Fransen. He had money, and he had brains, and he had vision. "I plan to stay here and put down roots," he told them at a banquet given in his honor. "Saboba can be the metropolis of the West and we, here in this room tonight, will be the cornerstones of a new culture." If there had been some who doubted Fransen's sincerity they were quashed that night. Men bragged of calling him by his first name and women vied with each other for the honor of having Mr. Fransen to supper.

Ross Parnell got up and put another stick of wood in the kitchen stove. "How did old Tuck Brant take it all?" he asked.

The judge stared into the wink of fire that escaped from around the edges of the stove door. An old man, lost in dreams of what might have been. A man who had once been powerful, both physically and mentally; a machine that was beginning to wear. Reactions were slower; the darkness of pessimism was beginning to take the luster off the brightness of his natural enthusiasm. A man, Ross thought, who has bumped his head on too many stars. "Tuck Brant." The judge repeated the name. "How did he take it all?"

"Nonsense, bushwah, and hogwash," Tuck Brant had said. "I been drivin' cows to a railroad for twenty years, and I don't need no damn railroad comin' around stinkin' up my place, scarin' my heifers so they throw their calves a month early. To hell with 'em. I'll shoot the first damn railroadman puts his foot on the XR."

But it seemed it was not so easy as that. The railroad kept pushing its way south and west, and Tuck Brant was smart enough to know that he was not big enough to stop it. So he licked his wounds and rumbled his threats, and out of the east came a new ally to secure his sovereignty. Barbed wire—devil rope, good stout posts from the breaks of the Sasinaw; four strands of wire without a gate in it. He'd fence in the XR and everything in that latitude, clear out to the escarpment. Then let the railroad bring its damned farmers; they'd never touch Tuck Brant inside his fortress of devil rope. Let Judge Iverson and those two-bit maverickers who called themselves cowmen be a part of this town if they chose. "Hell," bragged Tuck Brant, "I fence in my north line, and they'll all starve in six months. They've always lived off my beef." It wasn't so, and there were many who knew it. They kept still; men didn't argue with Tuck Brant.

So, instead, Saboba ignored Tuck Brant and his plan of isolation. Men could even joke about the XR. "When we're big as Chicago," one said, "we'll charge admission to the XR range. 'Right this way, folks. See the old West as she was!'"

Ben Fransen had opened a bank then, the judge remembered. He loaned money freely and no man complained of the interest. It took money to make money—that was the credo by which men lived these days. Everyone borrowed lavishly, mortgaging his land to the hilt, spending against calf crops not yet conceived. Even canny Dan Murdock decided it was time to build a new barn, and Don Diego Palomar, a child of a man with little concern for legal papers, mortgaged beyond his limit. Gib Baudry, too, dipped his fingers in the golden pie. But the worst offender was Ed Tozier, whining, complaining, never successful; at last here was a chance to measure up to the stability of his neighbor, Judge Iverson, a chance to match the social grandeur of Don Diego, whose ranch was there to the west. Ed Tozier went to Ben Franzen.

Then the day that was still known as Black Wednesday in Saboba. The judge sighed deeply and pounded the knuckles of his right hand into the palm of his left. "I should have known it would happen, Ross," he said softly. "I *must* have known it would happen. I didn't borrow like the others did; I didn't make crazy investments. Yet I didn't try to stop the others. Why, Ross? My town, Saboba; my people who live here. It's been that way, and I've wanted it that way. Call it conceit if you wish, but it has been my life. And until then they all came to me, Ross, just as you came to me when Tuck Brant fired you. Dan Murdock—Don Diego—Ed Tozier. Even Gib Baudry and Loop Fenton came to me, and at first I thought they were going to be all right. I'm still willing to give Baudry a chance."

It had come as quickly and as devastatingly as the northers which sometimes swept across the plains, the judge said: Tuck Brant was found with a bullet hole in the back of his head; found on the south bank of the Sasinaw, just below Ed Tozier's line; found by a ripped-up post of his new north-line fence, there in the mud-spattered and hoof-torn trail where a hundred head of cattle had been driven north.

Invincible, unbeatable Tuck Brant—dead by a rustler's bullet. And while the town and the plains hung in stunned immobility, Ben Fransen brought word that the railroad had turned and would miss Saboba by thirty miles. The cardboard house began to crumble, and neighbor turned against neighbor. A man called Kelly stole a cow to feed his family. An XR puncher sought out Kelly and shot him and left him lying there on the plains. The rustling raids grew bigger and bigger, and the XR drew up, ready for war.

But Ben Fransen stayed, and he worked like a gleaner in the leavings of destruction. Deserted stores became his by foreclosure; he took the biggest, and expanded the saloon and gambling house that had made him rich during the short months of the fat times, expanded while all others retreated. And again he was right, for men who could not find a dollar for a shirt could find a dollar for drinks to help dull the sting of the shortage. Payments on mortgages which Fransen held on the small cattle ranches north of the XR were met somehow and Fransen said he was glad about it, but it didn't ring true.

No longer did women have Ben Fransen to supper; no longer did men brag about being able to call him by his first name. Ben Fransen became a menace that hovered constantly over the town of Saboba. A menace who, if backed by one poor season, could wipe out a half-dozen ranches. It was Herbert Warrington who kept him from doing it.

Until now Warrington had kept apart, as much of a misfit as God had ever planted on a piece of land. When he rode at all it was in tight-legged breeches on a postage-stamp saddle, perched on the back of a bay Tennessee walking horse. When he tried to give orders to the XR crew, they laughed in his face. And in time it began to be whispered around that even Lenore had lost all respect for the dude she had married.

Then Warrington did the one thing that most men said proved he was crazy. He hired Ben Fransen's surveyors to recheck every line of the XR, and when he found that all that land lying between Catclaw Creek and the escarpment had never been legally purchased by Tuck Brant, Herbert Warrington himself was the first to admit it, and he openly said it was good land and invited the half-starved farmers who came here on the railroad dream to settle it and farm it. Ben Fransen took over the task of locating these farmers.

And now that the railroad was no longer coming this way the vast tract of plains south of the XR donated by the state became railroad land offered for sale. Ben Fransen bought section after section at twenty-five cents an acre. And Herbert Warrington, with the bright eyes of a fanatic, kept talking of wheat—billowing acres of wheat that would dwarf the cattle industry and make the XR an outmoded piece of the past, stumbling blindly through cow dung in the center of prosperity.

"A pretty picture," Ross Parnell said softly.

A door opened, and Maria stood there, a wrapper pulled tightly around her bulging frame. She glared, first at the judge, and then at Ross Parnell. She said, "Two pelados, both of you. Don't you gonna get no sleep? Half hour more and the sun is come up. You think you are hoot owls? Sit up all night; now you gonna lay around and sleep all day while I try to clean the house." She started toward a broom.

The judge said, "Now, Maria, calm down. We had a lot to talk over."

"Always talk," the housekeeper snorted.

"We'll get out of your way," Ross offered.

Maria reached out and pushed Ross back in his chair, hard. "You stay here. I gonna fix you some breakfast. You think I want you sick all over the place? Sometimes I think you crazy."

She slammed stove lids, pumped water into the coffee-pot, banged skillets and pots until the room was laced with noise. Outside, a rooster crowed lustily and Maria smiled. "You hear this?" she said, cocking her head. "Panchito! A rooster supposed to wake up the people, no? Every morning I wake up Panchito. Now he gonna wake up the rest of the chickens, and they wake up the rest of the town."

It seemed she was right. Panchito crowed again, and across town there was a lusty answer, then a half-dozen more, from as many compass points. A dog barked; a man chopped wood. Somewhere an old man started his morning coughing. And slowly Saboba shook off its sleep, and looked out at the river haze and the first spirals of wood smoke.

Leisurely, with nothing to say, Judge Iverson and Ross

Parnell had the breakfast of bacon and eggs and fried potatoes that Maria fixed for them. There were a lot of things for Ross to think about, and he thought of them clearly as a man does when the taste of coffee is in his mouth and the sting of sleeplessness in his eyes. He saw now that he had played with more than a gambler when he had matched cards with Ben Fransen. He had still not mentioned his winnings nor his encounter with Trip Levitt to the judge. He told himself it was because he did not want to burden the judge with personal affairs.

Ross could see now why the judge had been anxious to greet the Hedleys. The association that included Dan Murdock, Don Diego Palomar, Ed Tozier, and Gib Baudry could stand some reinforcements from a good solid citizen who was honestly bent on building up a ranch. Ross winced when he thought of that, remembering the plans of Sam Hedley and the rashness of Bret.

And immediately with that thought came a crazy, wild vision that had nothing to do with the affairs at hand. Perhaps he had dozed. Perhaps a tired brain plays tricks. He lifted his cup to his lips, and his eyes fell on the vacant chair directly across from him. For just a split second there was a perfect image of Jean Hedley, sitting there, watching him. She was smiling, and her eyes were soft and languorous, like the eyes of a woman who is happy. She was sweet with sleep. Ross set the cup down unsteadily. The judge looked at him queerly, with those cool, penetrating eyes that seemed to decipher every line of a man's thoughts. Ross coughed nervously and started to build a cigarette. The vision was gone.

And on the heels of it came a clamor of hoofbeats in the street and the shouting voice of Don Diego Palomar, more startling because Don Diego was a man of dignity. They could hear the slamming of doors, the quick screech as windows opened, and then the garbled calling back and forth, the speculation of the meaning of the early-morning intrusion. They heard the horse slide to a stop in front of the judge's house, and both Judge Iverson and Ross got to their feet and hurred to the front door. A cold, clammy apprehension fingered on Ross's spine, but he could not have said why.

They could see Don Diego Palomar, small, wiry, silver-haired, with a beautifully waxed mustache that matched; skin the color of coffee with cream. The little man was running up the walkway, frantically waving his arms. Maria had come to join Ross and the judge.

Por Dios, Señor Jefe! Ed Tozier se muerto! Madre de Dios!" The spouting stream of Spanish became completely unintelligible to Ross.

"Calm down now," the judge said, his voice sharp.

The Mexican rancher didn't slow his speech. And when he had finished he stood there, wringing his hands, a child of a man, and neither Ross nor the judge knew what he had said. Then they saw Maria, her face strangely pale. She looked from one man to the other and shook her head. Softly she said, "It is very bad news. I think. Don Diego say there is trouble on the north fence again. A hundred XR cattle have been driven north and Ed Tozier, he has been killed."

10

THE SULLEN town of Saboba stirred uneasily with a restless tension, as if the words of Maria had been heard in every house and every building from the north bank of the Sasinaw to the meanest hovel in Hogtown. A wind that came from the north touched the cottonwoods and set the leaves to whispering among themselves. The news that Don Diego had brought passed from tightly drawn mouth to anxious ear and was distorted by the arch of an eyebrow, a dilating of pupils, or the flare of nostrils.

Within the hour it was said that the XR was massing fifty riders for an all-out war against its neighbors, and when sleep-rested children went out to play, mothers spatted them back into the house. Men took stock of themselves as if to determine which side they favored. A feeling as ancient as life itself touched some—the tonic of war.

Judge Iverson, a jurist now, calmly and deliberately quizzed the excitable Don Diego Palomar; the answers he got were sparse, nearly hysterical. It had come in the time between midnight and dawn, perhaps three o'clock, Don Diego said. Ross Parnell calculated back and saw that it was about the time he had left Ben Fransen's.

Four XR punchers who had rowdied the night in Hogtown were riding home by the river trail, as Don Diego reconstructed it. It was near the point where the river bowed to the north and cornered Ed Tozier's land to bear east again across the Iverson place and the outskirts of Saboba. These men had heard the bawl of cattle and the shout of riders. The night was inky dark, but from the lay of the land and the direction taken it was not hard to see that the stolen herd was being hazed across the breaks into Ed Tozier's pastures.

Perhaps ten men were with the cattle. It was too dark to see who they were, but one might have been Ed Tozier himself. The XR men opened fire. The rustlers answered the challenge and there was an exchange of perhaps a dozen shots, but because of the darkness and the plunging of the horses no one was hit. Of this the XR punchers were sure.

The sound of the gunshots had come plainly to the house of Don Diego. He had called the three vaqueros who rode for him, and, barring the door, had left them there to protect his wife; then he had ridden quickly on the trail that followed the breaks to the house of his friend, Ed Tozier. On the trail he found Ed Tozier dead, with a bullet in the back of his head.

This was the story Don Diego Palomar brought to Judge Iverson, and the little rancher's voice was distraught with grief and anxiety, yet his recital was touched with a spark of indignation and vengeance. He twisted his hands in a manner peculiar to him, and said, "For the years I have lived here the XR has wanted trouble. Tuck Brant himself, and now his daughter. And tonight they have found a way. The story of the cattle and night riders—could it not be a lie, Señor Judge? Could it not be that these XR men who rode from Hogtown by the river trail drove the cattle themselves, and took our friend Ed Tozier from his bed and murdered him? Loop Fenton was killed, and perhaps we judged too soon. Perhaps the words of his wife were true. We did not go to war, so now the XR has tried again, and this time they have killed our friend of many years. A harmless man who in a dispute would brand a calf of his own with the XR rather than make a mistake. A man who wanted the north fence more than any of us. It is because of this they chose to murder him."

"A man has a right to his thoughts, Don Diego," Judge Iverson said softly, "but we'll accomplish nothing by losing our heads. I've sent boys for Dan Murdock and Gib Baudry. We'll talk this over calmly."

"And while we do?" the little Mexican fretted. "If the XR have planned this war they have called in their men from the line camps and from the fence crew. They can put fifty fighting men in the saddle while we sit and talk calmly. We have been friends for years, Señor Judge, and always I have respected your decisions. But now, if it must be war, I am not one who fights guns with words. I have three vaqueros of my own; Dan Murdock has four. On Ed Tozier's place his three riders have already put on their guns, for are they not accused of rustling by the XR?

At your own North Ranch I know of five men who will do as you say. Gib Baudry has many friends in Hogtown."

Don Diego had made up his mind, Ross could see. For years the Mexican had been harassed by Tuck Brant, and in the eyes of the XR owner his unwelcome neighbor had never risen beyond the rank of "cholo." Ross could remember when Palomar's accepted range had reached south nearly to the XR headquarters. Gradually it had been pushed back, north of the river, then north of Cache Creek, and finally beyond the breaks. It had not been land that Don Diego had owned except by squatters' rights; section by section Tuck Brant had bought it up and legally pushed back the boundaries of the proud, small Rancho Los Lobos. But the fiery temper of the Latin had not forgotten; Don Diego Palomar was ready to fight. Yesterday Gib Baudry had been ready to avenge the death of Loop Fenton, a known rustler; this affair today would add fuel to his determination. And Dan Murdock was a solid man, with a mind of his own, and the disposition of a scorpion once he was aroused.

Judge Iverson was an old man now, a man who had lost much of his power since the coming of Ben Fransen. His honor and his integrity no man could doubt, but he had reached the point where some were saying the old flame was gone. "There's no more of the fight and fire in the man," they said. "He likes to sit at home and bake his shins and talk of brotherhood and compromise. Where's this great city of Saboba he talked of? Where's the railroad that was going to make us rich?"

It was past time for the sun now, but the sun was not there. The sky was a leaden, solid sheet, drawn tightly around the wide circle of the horizon. Against that sheet the tension and violence of men struck like ice pellets on a tin roof, rebounded, grew in number, and piled up. Saboba was a hive of violence waiting for a misinterpreted word, an accidental gunshot. A fist fight between strangers broke out on the corner by Jim East's saloon.

Dan Murdock arrived. There was a six-shooter belted around his middle, and there was a rifle in his saddle boot. He brought three armed riders with him; they dismounted and sat with their backs against the judge's fence while their boss went inside. The riders made cigarettes, and smoked thoughtfully, and watched the street.

Gib Baudry, his face still showing the marks of Ross's fists, came and talked to Dan Murdock's riders. He strode up and down in front of them, and twice he stopped to shake his fist.

Suddenly it seemed to Ross that this thing had a plan, and was not merely the consummation of years of distrust and dislike between the XR and its small neighbors; it had moved too quickly, too violently. He remembered Ben Fransen's words of the night before. "I made a mistake and located a couple of settlers between the Catclaw and the escarpment out there at the east end of the XR range. I been hoping they'd get discouraged and go back to Kansas." Fransen had been merely feeling him out, Ross knew, trying to see what his reaction would be to a proposition. But suppose Fransen had tried it on someone else and had found the reaction he wanted? Carrying it a step further, suppose Fransen had said then, "I've been hoping Ed Tozier would give up his place."

Ross felt a coldness between his shoulder blades. Bret Hedley had been to see Ben Fransen. Fransen said the kid sounded like somebody with sense. Ross tried to shake it off, angry at himself for letting the thought enter his mind. He didn't like Bret Hedley, hadn't from the first, and this thought was merely a devil of vindictiveness that had come unbidden—a dart of viciousness such as touches the thoughts of any man. There were fifty men in Hogtown who could be hired to kill. But he found it was not Bret he was trying to protect by changing his thinking: again that picture of Jean had been strong in his mind.

Judge Iverson, his voice soft, pleading, almost pathetically inadequate in the face of the situation, was trying to reason with Dan Murdock and Don Diego Palomar. Murdock said, "A speech gets tiresome once you've heard it a dozen times, Judge. I've heard yours twenty times."

Gib Baudry came in without knocking. He stood there in the middle of the room, bareheaded, sleeves rolled back off his underwear. A barrel of a man, with a shaggy, brutish head, and small animal eyes, a broad, flat nose. He blurted, "Well, dammit, if you had listened to me yesterday, we'd a had the jump on 'em. I told you it meant war, and you wouldn't listen. Still gonna fight fire with honey, Judge?" There was nothing subtle about Gib Baudry. He was anxious to see this thing start, almost too anxious.

Ross said, "You've got a habit of pushing things, Baudry."

Gib swiveled his head slowly; his neck seemed to telescope down, bringing his chin closer to his chest. His shoulders hunched, and his arms bowed slightly. He said, "You got a habit of buttin' into affairs that ain't none of your damn business. Who asked you to this party, Parnell?"

"I did." Judge Iverson's voice was sharp, uncompromising.

Dan Murdock, a ponderous man, slow-thinking, said, "Hold on a minute, Judge. I sort of string along with Gib on that. I got nothin' personal against Ross, but we're layin' ourselves open for a lot of trouble if we bring in outside gun help."

Ross flushed darkly. "I hadn't figured on hiring out my gun," he said.

"Now don't get your tail up," Murdock insisted. He spoke slowly, as if thinking out each phrase. "I told you

I had nothing against you personally and I meant it. But there's folks hereabouts we'd like on our side—and who in hell don't know why you came back to Saboba? You left here wearin' a gun, Ross, and you come back the same way."

The man was right, Ross knew, but it didn't ease the sting. Judge Iverson kept pacing up and down the room, not meeting Ross's eyes. Diego Palomar, his sensitive face set and hard, said, "We have friends in the new settlers there across the Catclaw, Ross. They wouldn't understand." The little Mexican shrugged his shoulders. "It is true you are thought of as an XR man. The settlers have had trouble with the XR. Perhaps they will have more."

Judge Iverson turned quickly, his face drawn by the conflict that was going on within him. A few years back, and his word would have been enough. Now he said, "There's no need of you getting yourself mixed up in this thing, boy."

. "Forget it." Ross said, biting off the words. "I was just passin' through."

The judge went to a closet and got the gun belt and the cedar-butt .44. He handed it over to Ross and said, "Good luck, boy. You're always welcome here."

Ross buckled the gun around his middle, and, turning a slow gaze on each man in turn, he said, "So long, boys." He stopped in the door, half-turned, and to Gib Baudry he said, "By the way, Gib, did you ever finish that business with Ben Fransen?"

He didn't wait to see the big man's reaction. He went down the walk and through the gate; when he came to where Dan Murdock's men still waited, one of them got up and threw away his cigarette. Ross shifted the gun to a more comfortable position.

The old feeling was strong in him now, just as it had been that day when Tuck Brant had thrown him off the XR. It was not a feeling of resentment, nor particularly of wounded pride. Rather, it was a gnawing inadequacy that settled some place in the pit of his stomach and ground away at his vitals and said over and over "You don't amount to much, Ross Parnell. You don't amount to a damn. You're a pelado." When a man got that feeling, it was time to drink. Or, maybe, ride.

As far back as he could remember, he had been a part of this country and yet he had never been a part of anything. His parents had died far enough back that he remembered them only slightly; there was a dim picture in his mind of a tall, rangy man with a certain slowness about him, a man of little ambition and no accomplishments. The memory of his mother was even less vivid. There was nothing to hold him.

So, when the press came, he had drifted, and it seemed a natural and easy thing to do. For five years now he had drifted, a saddle tramp. But he overlooked the fact that in doing it he was trying to run from himself. And, too, he had overlooked his feeling for Lenore Brant, a feeling he could neither explain nor overcome. The other item was the fact that he had left a gun job half done, a gun job that had not been of his making.

These were the things that had brought him back to the only home he had known, and he had expected Saboba to greet him and welcome him. He laughed now, a short, hard laugh. He tried to give himself one good reason why Saboba should accept him. He thought of Ben Fransen, a good man to know, and he headed toward the saloon. There were only two men at the long bar. One was Ben Fransen himself; the other was Bret Hedley.

He couldn't tell what it was, but seeing Bret there gave him a quick stab of uneasiness. He thought of the calm, calculating coolness of Ben Fransen and the quick, uncontrollable temper of young Bret, and he didn't like the combination. Strangely, he still felt a halfway obligation toward Bret; he couldn't quite forget the way Jean had asked him to look out for the kid. He moved down next to them, pushed his hat back on his head, and ordered a bottle. Fransen said, "Lost your money yet, Parnell?"

"Not yet," Ross said.

Bret Hedley said nothing. He took a drink, too fast, as if perhaps he wasn't used to drinking, Ross noticed the kid was wearing his gun. Bret poured himself another drink, spilling some of the liquor. He made a cigarette, and his hands trembled. Fransen said, "Taking sides in this thing?"

"Haven't decided," Ross said.

"I wouldn't want to be riding with Tony Sellew."

"More advice, Fransen?"

"Just conversation."

They stood there that way, feeling each other out. Fransen was cool and sure, Ross merely putting out feelers, trying to see the direction of the wind without becoming too involved. Bret's nervousness increased constantly, as if Ross and Fransen were getting ready to close in on him. Looking straight into the mirror, not turning his head, Ross said, "How's your maw feeling, Bret?"

Bret didn't answer.

"The Hedleys are buying up the Tozier place," said Ben Fransen.

Ross waited a long time, until he was sure he could conceal his surprise. "Good place," he said. His eyes moved slightly in the mirror now, and studied Bret's face. It was strained, pale, like the face of a man who has had no sleep and been under too much strain. There was a long rip in the sleeve of the leather jacket he wore. Ross said, "Up late last night, was you, Bret?"

Bret turned quickly, his voice high, strident. "You ain't gonna bait me into no damn fight!"

"Who's trying to?" Ross said. He still hadn't turned his head.

Fransen said, "I held quite a mortgage on Tozier's place. He's got no relatives to take over, so I picked it up."

"It was convenient of Ed to get killed," Ross said.

A muscle at one corner of Bret Hedley's mouth began to twitch. He downed another drink, then pushed himself back from the bar. He stood there, and with the twist of rage and fear that was on his face he seemed even younger than he was. He said, "Say what you mean, Parnell."

Ross met the kid's gaze, held it a long second. There was a half-smile on his face. He shrugged his shoulders and said, "As Fransen says, just conversation."

There was perspiration on Bret Hedley's upper lip. He said, "Stay out of my way, Parnell."

Ross grinned. "Forget it, kid," he said. "I'm going over to the hotel and get me some sleep. You could do with the same."

11

NIGHT BEFORE last, out there at the fence line, Ross had had little sleep; last night there had been none. And yet as he stretched out on the bed in the hotel room across the street from Fransen's he found that sleep was refusing to come. There was a mounting tension in the town that seemed to charge the air, but beyond that there was a tension in himself that kept growing, until he got up, made himself a cigarette, and paced back and forth across the room.

Once he went to the window and looked out on the street. He could see a couple of XR riders coming in, riding side by side, slowly. They dismounted in front of Fransen's, and went inside. Ross ground the cigarette between his thumb and forefinger and threw it on the floor. Before he realized what he was doing he had made another. He took the package of paper money out of his shirt front, ran through it hurriedly, replaced it.

This whole thing had too much plan about it, too much precision. There was no way of figuring just where Ben Fransen stood in it, but of one thing Ross was nearly certain. Ben Fransen knew who killed Ed Tozier; he must have had his reasons for not saying. Again he thought of Bret, and he tried to put the idea aside as impossible. Bret was just a kid—he couldn't be hired to kill a man. The argument wasn't convincing.

He slept finally, a fitful sleep that was broken each time a board creaked, each time a man spoke too loudly down there on the street. Something awakened him completely and he went to the window again, his heart beating hard as it does when a man is startled into wakefulness. It was nearly dusk, and in front of Fransen's, Tony Sellew was talking to a half-dozen XR men. Tony was standing on the porch, and Ross could catch his words clearly. "Check your guns, boys, all of you. We're not looking for trouble. The sheriff's out at Tozier's now and he'll handle things." It was too pat a speech, too loud. Ross remembered the hide-out gun Sellew carried, and wondered how many more such guns were with that crew.

He gave up trying to sleep, and, pouring a basin full of water, he washed his face and sloshed cold water over the back of his head. After that he combed his hair carefully with the comb that hung on a string beside the cracked mirror. Rubbing an exploring palm across his cheek, he decided to get himself a shave before eating. He went downstairs and out on the street. Sellew, still on the porch, called to him, "Hi, Lucky! Still around?"

"Still around," said Ross. He saw Dan Murdock farther down the block, knew that the rancher had heard the greeting. He went up the street and found a barbershop and while he was waiting he decided to have a bath and a haircut as well as a shave. The barber motioned him toward the curtained-off back room and Ross went inside.

There was a small tin tub. Four galvanized buckets of steaming water sat on a lustily burning wood stove. A hand pump that drained into a V-shaped trough passing out through the wall into the alley furnished the tempering cold water. Ross undressed and poured a bucket of the hot water into the tub.

He was in the tub and had lathered himself as well as he could with the yellow soap and the hard water when the curtain moved aside and Tony Sellew came into the steamy room. Ross went on scrubbing, not paying much attention to his visitor, wondering what had brought the XR foreman here. Sellew took a pocketknife from his pocket, opened the blade, and started paring his fingernails. He said finally, "What do you know, Parnell?"

"About what?"

"You spent some time with the judge and the others. Who they figure killed Ed Tozier?"

"They didn't say," Ross said truthfully.

"You got any ideas?"

"I might have."

Sellew snapped the knife shut, tossed it in the air, and caught it with a down sweep of his hand. He said, "Why don't you come on back to work for the XR, Ross? I said before I could use a good hand. I don't mean plantin' wheat."

"I'll think about it," Ross promised.

"See you at Fransen's later?"

"After I eat."

Sellew left, and Ross thought, "Now what the hell did he want?" He went on scrubbing thoughtfully; when he was through and dressed, he checked the loads in his six-shooter before buckling the belt around his middle. He took the money from his boot, where he had stuffed it, and replaced it in his shirt front. The shop was deserted now, so he had a shave and haircut and then went next door to the restaurant, where he had a steak and fried potatoes. The man behind the counter said, "I don't like it a damn bit, mister, not a damn bit. There's gonna be hell to pay before it's over."

"The XR left their guns off," Ross said.

"You an XR man?"

"Some say so."

"I don't take sides in the damn thing," the counterman said. "I buy my beefsteaks and there ain't no way of tellin' where they come from. I don't take no side at all."

He went outside and ran into Judge Iverson hurrying along the sidewalk. The judge said, "I been looking for you, Ross. About this morning."

"Forget it, Judge," Ross said, removing the toothpick from his mouth and tossing it aside. "How's it coming along?"

"Diego Palomar and Gib Baudry have gone out to talk to the Warringtons. We're going to try to work out an arrangement where we'll give notes for half the expense on that north fence to show good faith——"

Ross interrupted, "How'd you happen to let Gib Baudry go?"

The judge spread his hands. "I'm outvoted, Ross." Ross didn't like hearing him say it: it was like hearing an old man say, "I've lived my life now—I'm through."

"You think they'll go ahead with the fence?" Ross asked.

"They've got to," the judge said. "Either that or we all go under. You can't keep cows out of those breaks without a fence, and on open range like that there's bound to be mix-ups. Beyond that there's always been rustling along the Sasinaw and for all I know there always will be. A fence will at least stop these wholesale raids and keep us from accusing each other." The judge sounded more like himself now.

"Hope they go for it, Judge," Ross said sincerely. "Too bad you had to send Baudry."

"I would like to have sent you, Ross."

"I've decided to drift along," Ross said.

"And Trip Levitt?"

"We've got to meet up someday. I'll try to make it soon."

"You're getting old enough to settle down."

"It's not for me."

They shook hands, and Ross went on down the street and turned in at Ben Fransen's saloon. He still hadn't told the judge about his winnings nor about his meeting with Trip Levitt, and now he felt a twinge of guilt about it. It had been good, seeing old Maria again, sitting there last night in the judge's kitchen. He remembered how he had thought of Jean Hedley while he was sitting there, having his coffee, and to himself he said, "It's not for me." He went inside the saloon, and the quick wash of cheap perfume, whisky, sweaty men, and cigarette smoke was hot in his nostrils. Unconsciously his hand touched the bulge in his shirt where he had concealed the money. The roulette wheel set up a musical chatter.

But he didn't gamble. He went to a table alone, and ordered a bottle, and he poured the first drink hurriedly. The liquor was not good on top of the food he had just eaten, and in some way he felt guilty about drinking it. He smoked a cigarette to take away the sting of the raw whisky and suddenly he was looking himself square in the eye and he didn't like what he saw. "You're feeling sorry for yourself, Parnell," he thought. "You're a weak sister." He had another drink.

He saw Tony Sellew across the room in a poker game. The look on the XR foreman's face said he was losing

**Enjoy the Best
of the World's Bestselling
Frontier Storyteller in...**

THE
LOUIS L'AMOUR
COLLECTION

**Savor <u>Silver Canyon</u> in this new hardcover
collector's edition free for 10 days.**

At last, a top-quality, hardcover edition of the
best frontier fiction of Louis L'Amour. Beautifully
produced books with hand-tooled covers, gold-
leaf stamping, and double-sewn bindings.

Reading and rereading these books will give
you hours of satisfaction. These are works of
lasting pleasure. Books you'll be proud to pass
on to your children.

MEMO FROM LOUIS L'AMOUR

Dear Reader:

Over the years, many people have asked me when a first-rate hardcover collection of my books would become available. Now the people at Bantam Books have made that hope a reality. They've put together a collection of which I am very proud. Fine bindings, handsome design, and a price which I'm pleased to say makes these books an affordable addition to almost everyone's permanent library.

Bantam Books has so much faith in this series that they're making what seems to me is an extraordinary offer. They'll send you Silver Canyon, on a 10-day, free examination basis. Plus they'll send you a free copy of my new Calendar.

Even if you decide for any reason whatever to return Silver Canyon, you may keep the Calendar free of charge and without obligation. Personally, I think you'll be delighted with Silver Canyon and the other volumes in this series.

Sincerely,

Louis L'Amour

Louis L'Amour

P.S. They tell me supplies of the Calendar are limited, so you should order now.

Take Advantage Today of This No-Risk, No-Obligation Offer

You'll enjoy these features:

- An heirloom-quality edition
- An affordable price
- Gripping stories of action and adventure
- A $6.95 calendar yours free while supplies last just for examining <u>Silver Canyon</u>
- No minimum purchase; no obligation to purchase even one volume.

Pre-Publication Reservation

( ) YES! Please send me the new collector's edition of <u>Silver Canyon</u> for a 10-day free examination upon publication, along with my free Louis L'Amour Calendar, and enter my subscription to <u>The Louis L'Amour Collection</u>. If I decide to keep <u>Silver Canyon</u>, I will pay $7.95 plus shipping and handling. I will then receive additional volumes in the Collection at the rate of one volume per month on a fully return-able, 10-day, free-examination basis. There is no minimum number of books I must buy, and I may cancel my subscription at any time.

05066

If I decide to return <u>Silver Canyon</u>, I will return the book within 10 days, my subscription to <u>The Louis L'Amour Collection</u> will expire, and I will have no additional obligation. The Calendar is mine to keep in any case.

( ) **I would prefer the deluxe edition, bound in genuine leather, to be billed at only $24.95 plus shipping and handling.**

05074

Name _____

Address _____

City _____ State _____ Zip _____

This offer is good for a limited time only. Supplies of calendar are limited.

K 0

BUSINESS REPLY MAIL

FIRST CLASS   PERMIT NO. **2154**   HICKSVILLE, N.Y.

POSTAGE WILL BE PAID BY

THE LOUIS L'AMOUR COLLECTION

BANTAM BOOKS
P.O. BOX 956
HICKSVILLE, NEW YORK 11801

and was covering his loss with too much liquor. The girl,
Queenie, came by and stopped at Sellew's table. He
shoved her aside and started to deal the cards. Ross saw
her say something, curt, angry. Sellew said, loud enough
for Ross to hear, "Get the hell out of here." The girl
went up on the little stage and started to sing. The piano
player caught the tune with one hand while he finished
his beer. Ben Fransen came to the head of the stairs,
looked over the gaming tables, then went back. Ross made
up his mind. The hell with it. He was getting out.

Queenie finished her song and came down off the stage.
She didn't go toward Tony Sellew's table this time but
instead wormed her way through the crowd with her
peculiar undulating walk, brushing men with her hips
as she passed. She went toward the back of the room, beyond the dice tables, and then Ross saw him—Bret Hedley. He was wearing his gun, and had been drinking more
than his share. Dan Murdock was at the table with him.
Queenie stood by the table talking, and Bret reached up,
got her around the waist, and pulled her down on his
lap. She laughed, and it carried above the noise. Tony
Sellew glanced up from his cards, frowned, then resumed
playing.

At the end of the bar one man shoved another and an
argument started. There was a quick quiet; Sellew said,
"Watch it, Rex." The man who had done the shoving
turned back to his drink.

A little thing, as small as that, and yet it reminded men
that the powder keg was still here. Conversations rose
and fell rapidly and sometimes they died completely.
Queenie got up from the table and started to sing Sellew's song:

"Take back the ring you gave me—"

Bret Hedley's voice was sharp, a little whisky-thick.
"Come over here and sit on my lap and sing it, baby. I

like to feel you breathing." Tony Sellew laid down his
cards. Queenie looked across the room, saw Tony, then
stepped down from the stage and walked directly to
Bret's table. She sat on his lap, put her arm around his
neck, tilted his chin with her hand and kissed him on the
lips. To the piano player she said, "Start it over, Briggs."
Her voice was soft and vibrant now, half-muffled against
Bret's cheek.

> *"Take back the ring you gave me——"*

Ross knew it was coming before it ever started. He
heard the scrape of the chair and then the rattle of chips
as they spilled from the table. Sellew, weaving a little, got
up and started pushing his way through the tables. The
girl must have seen him coming, but she continued with
her singing, hiding Bret's eyes, now, against her naked
chest.

> *"So please take it back, I beg of you, Jack——"*

Sellew's voice was harsh. "Cut it out, Queenie."
Bret straightened suddenly, shaking his head to focus
his eyes. He said, "What the hell?"
Sellew reached out, took Queenie by the wrist, and
jerked her off Bret's lap. He slapped her then, hard, and,
as she stepped back away from the blow, she tripped
against a chair and fell. Bret was on his feet, his face red,
his eyes wicked. Chairs upset and men spilled aside. Dan
Murdock was up, backing Bret. A half-dozen XR punchers moved away from the bar. Murdock's three riders
came and took their place by their boss. There wasn't a
gun in sight except the one Bret wore.
This was it, the thing they had waited for all day.
Nothing could stop it now; it had to break. Ross thought
of one thing only—that hide-out gun he knew Sellew was

wearing. The minute a blow was landed, all hell would cut loose, and in the bedlam that followed someone was going to get hurt. He had seen the hot flare of jealousy in Tony Sellew before; it was augmented now by whisky and raw nerves. Bret was wearing a gun, and Tony would have a perfect excuse for going for his own. As instinctively as he had moved back there at the arroyo when he had heard Jean's scream, Ross moved now. He pushed aside his table, knocked over two chairs, slid by Tony Sellew, and his fist landed solidly on Bret's chin. The kid went down without knowing what had hit him.

It started: there was a gunshot, and the room was in darkness; Queenie screamed, over and over; somewhere there was a thud of fists, and a man cursed violently. Bodies began intermingling, and from out of the darkness a fist grazed Ross's head, knocking him to his knees. He crawled forward, and found Bret there on the floor.

Outside the town had heard the first echoes of the fight and now there was a tumult of sound, the sudden hoofbeats of horses cut loose from their hitch rails. A shotgun blasted, a deep double-barreled roar, and the shot pinged against the walls. A warning shot from behind the bar. Someone pushed in close and Ross swung, knocking the man aside. He had no idea who it might have been. It cleared a path, and he stooped down and managed to get Bret over his shoulder.

He fought his way through, then, coming finally to the front door, being stopped there while he slugged it out with an unknown assailant. There was blood in his mouth and it was slippery on his hands. He got hold of Bret's feet and dragged him outside, into the air. The street was deserted, but as he stood there he heard three horses cross the bridge, coming at a dead run. They slid into the fan of lights that came from the hotel and restaurant and he recognized Diego Palomar and Gib Baudry. Riding with them was Lenore Warrington. She wore

those skin-tight Levis, the old sheepskin coat, and the
battered felt hat. There was a rifle in the saddle scabbard
beneath her right leg. She threw herself free of the saddle,
snaked out the rifle, and crossed the street. From the
other direction Judge Iverson, hatless, coatless, came on
a dead run, his long legs whipping him along. There
was another gunshot from inside the saloon, then a match
flickered and a lamp went up. Bret Hedley groaned and
pushed himself up off the board sidewalk. He started to
curse. Ross said, "Shut up, you damn fool! He had a
gun."

Inside the saloon someone was moaning horribly, and
another man kept cursing, over and over. Lenore, seeing
that Ross was wearing his gun, said, "Give me a hand.
I want my men out of there." He moved to her side
quickly, ignoring Bret, who was getting to his feet.

They pushed aside the door together, Ross and Lenore,
and they stood there side by side, Ross with a cocked six-
shooter in his hand, Lenore with the rifle. She spoke one
word: "Sellew!" It was like Tuck Brant would have said
it. Tony Sellew came out of the murky half-darkness.
"Get our men out of there, quick!"

Behind them on the street there was an agitated conversation going on, with Judge Iverson in the middle of
it. Ross heard a familiar voice and knew without looking
that it was Bill Yates, sheriff of Sasinaw County. He had
spent all day and half the night at the Tozier place, trying
to pick up some clue.

Lenore backed out of the doorway and lowered the
rifle, letting the barrel point toward the ground. A second before she had been in complete command, the
owner of the XR, the daughter of Tuck Brant. For a
second she had been more man than woman. And now,
just as suddenly, she was small, feminine, helpless: she
brushed the palm of her hand across her forehead; then
she turned and looked at Ross. Their glances held, and,

although he couldn't be sure, there might have been tears in the eyes of Lenore Warrington. She said, "We met the sheriff outside of town. He knows who killed Ed Tozier." There was a quick movement behind them, and Ross turned in time to see Bret Hedley inching out toward the horses that stood in the street.

12

IT MUST have been at that exact moment that Sheriff Bill Yates announced the name of Ed Tozier's killer. A dozen men saw Bret Hedley start toward the horses, and a dozen men moved forward, confused and held for a second by the knowledge that they were dealing with a murderer. The bewilderment of the fight was still everywhere, and tempers had not yet run out. No man knew where another man stood, and it was the break Bret Hedley needed.

He got to the horse, threw himself into the saddle, and fired two warning shots. Ross moved swiftly, pushing Lenore inside the saloon. Then his gun was out and he called once, "Hold it, Bret!"

The other men, with the exception of Judge Iverson, had made a quick dive for cover. The Judge stood there alone in the middle of the street, hatless, coatless, tall, imposing in his isolation. Bret wheeled the horse, sunk his spurs shank deep, and the animal reared. The judge made a grab for the bridle. The gun in Bret's hand came down in a wild swing, he was using it as a club. There was a flash, a roar, and then the horse was away and Judge Iverson was staggering toward the sidewalk, clutching at his chest. His steps became longer, more awkward, his body jerked, and he fell, his hand reaching out as if trying to find some support.

There was a quick moment of horrified silence. Ross

ran to the middle of the street and fired three shots at the horseman being swallowed up by the darkness. A woman screamed. The hysterical calling of a name. "Bret! Bret!" He half-turned and saw Jean Hedley running down the street. He caught her in his arms and held her face close to his shoulder just as he had done that day in the arroyo when she had seen Loop Fenton's body hanging from a limb.

A sudden confusion in the crowd that had formed on the sidewalk. Pushing and shoving, the quick curses of men. The sound of a fist thudding against flesh. Ross saw Lenore not six feet away. He led Jean to her and said only, "Take care of her." Then he pushed his way into the crowd that was milling there on the sidewalk. They had Sam Hedley in the middle of a circle. They were pushing him back and forth, slapping him, cursing him, kicking. Ross shoved his way through, got in front of the old man. He said, "Leave him alone."

He got Sam out in the clear and said, "Get Maw and Jean out of town, quick. Go on out to the Tozier place if that's where you were heading. You know about it?"

Sam looked like a man who was dazed, a man who had been beaten over the head. He said, "The sheriff come to us first. He was lookin' for Bret." He turned and started walking up the street in the direction of Hogtown.

Ross went to where a half-dozen white-faced men were kneeling at the side of Judge Iverson. He recognized Don Diego and Dan Murdock. He said, "Alive?" Someone nodded. Ross said, "Where the hell's the doctor?"

"Busy inside."

"Get him out here."

He felt the hard grip of a hand on his shoulder and he turned and saw Dan Murdock, his face void of color, his lips set. Murdock said, "Get on back with your XR crew, Parnell."

"Wait a minute, Dan."

"It was you sided Tony Sellew in that fight. It was you she called on to back her up with a gun. Stay the hell away from me, Parnell."

"Dan, listen——"

The big man's hand shot out and gripped Ross by the shirt front. His right fist came back. He said again, "Stay the hell away from me!" He shoved, and Ross stumbled back. The doctor came running out of the saloon, pushed his way between them. Don Diego Palomar and two of Murdock's men were on their knees beside the judge.

Lenore Warrington's voice said softly, "Shall we take her out to my place, Ross?" She was holding Jean, trying to quiet her sobbing.

Ross said, "She better be with her dad and maw. I'll take her."

He took Jean's hand and started leading her away from the crowd. She swayed toward him and her body went limp. He picked her up in his arms and carried her; she was as light as a child. He walked down the middle of the street alone, carrying her in his arms, and there was a hard, surging bitterness in him he had never felt before. A tenseness in his muscles, a determination that made him want to fight, even to kill.

He saw the old wagon coming across the slough from Hogtown and he hailed Sam, and together they put Jean inside, under the bowed canvas. Sam had that same fixed dazed expression on his face. Ross said, "She'll be all right, Sam. Go on out to Tozier's. I'll come by later."

Sam said, "I can't go. I've got to get me a doctor. It's Maw—she's back there with Agnes Fenton."

Ross said, "You've got to go, Sam; they'll turn on you. I'll take care of things here—I promise you I will."

Sam climbed back on the seat, still dazed, and the wagon started down the street. The sheriff cleared a way for him, and men moved aside and let the wagon pass.

Ross hurried over to Judge Iverson's to see if he could

get the doctor. He was met at the door by Gib Baudry and Dan Murdock. They both had rifles. Murdock said, "Stay away from here, Parnell."

Ross said, "I want the doctor."

Murdock tilted the rifle. He said, "Get out or I'll blow you in two."

Lenore Warrington came out of the shadows there at the edge of the porch. She put her hand on Ross's arm. "Come on, Ross," she said softly. "It's no use. I've tried to talk to them."

He pulled away from her touch roughly, then just as quickly said, "Will you go with me? Maw Hedley."

She said, "Yes, Ross. I'll go."

They went back onto the main street and turned toward Hogtown. Behind them men were still milling around in front of Fransen's, and he knew a posse was being formed to go after Bret Hedley.

They didn't speak, and at this moment they seemed more a part of each other than they had ever been. A part, as if each of them were alone and needed each other in that aloneness.

Hogtown was strangely silent as they walked past the bagnios, the dead-falls, and came to the Fenton shack that stood alone and barren in the middle of a lot. There was a single light burning in the front window. Agnes Fenton answered their knock. She had a shotgun in her hand.

Ross said, "We've come about Mrs. Hedley. To see if we could help."

Agnes Fenton's eyes were glassy bright. Her lips did not move when she spoke. She said, "She's dead. Get the hell out." The door slammed in their faces.

They stood there in the darkness, and without hearing himself say it he said, "Jean. What'll we do for her, Lenore? What'll we do for her?"

Lenore pressed his hand and said softly, "I understand, Ross."

They walked back then, saying nothing, to where Sheriff Bill Yates was making up his posse. Tony Sellew was there and a half-dozen XR riders, ready to ride with the sheriff. No one spoke to Ross Parnell nor to Lenore Warrington. Lenore said, "I've got to get back to the ranch, Ross. Ride with me, please. I don't want to go alone."

He said, "Wait here a minute."

He was hardly conscious of what was going on around him. He was only aware of that savage drive that was touching every muscle, every nerve in his body. He pushed open the doors of Fransen's saloon and went inside. The main room was a shambles; over in one corner, by the piano, Queenie was slouched in a chair, crying. He wanted to slap her face.

The bartenders and the dealers were moving around through the wreckage, righting a chair here, picking up an odd piece of broken glass, moving with a fixed orderliness, accomplishing nothing in the chaos. He stood there a moment, not planning, not knowing for sure what he was going to do. And then he turned to the stairway and went up slowly, deliberately, a step at a time. He counted the doors on the first landing and stopped at the fourth. He didn't knock, but reached down with his left hand and turned the knob. The door was open and he pushed it wide and stood there. Ben Fransen was standing at the far side of the room, a cigar clamped in his teeth, a gun thrust in the waistband of his trousers.

Fransen didn't remove the cigar. It bobbed up and down when he spoke. "What the hell do you want, Parnell?"

And everything that was inside him exploded then and centered on that cold piece of machinery that stood there across the room. There was no way, probably, in which guilt of any kind could be fastened on Ben Fransen. He was too clever for that. And yet everything Ross knew about the man was hot in his mind. The way he had taken over Saboba; the cold, calculating way in which he had let Ross know how he stood; his coldness and cleverness against the hot, young, impressionable mind of nineteen-year-old Bret Hedley. The killing of Ed Tozier. . . .

Fransen's hand moved toward the gun in his waistband. He said, "I asked you, what you want?"

Ross said, "This."

He made one quick lunge across the room, saw Fransen's hand jerk at the gun in his waistband. Ross's head caught the big man in the pit of the stomach.

Fransen slammed back against the wall, and Ross cocked his right fist, slashed in, and crushed his knuckles against the jaw of the saloonkeeper. Fransen went down hard and lay there. A small trickle of blood appeared at the corner of his mouth. It ran down the side of his chin.

Ross picked up his crumpled hat, straightened it, and put it back on his head. He turned, and went back outside, closing the door behind him. At the head of the stairs he paused. Below him, there, the dealers and the bartenders were still picking around through the rubble. He went downstairs and out through the door, and no one seemed to notice him. Lenore was waiting for him on the sidewalk. The posse had already ridden.

He said, "My horse is up at the stable. I'll ride with you."

At that precise moment he couldn't tell whether he loved her or hated her; there seemed to be a complete conflict between the two emotions. Somehow he thought of Herbert Warrington.

She got her horse and mounted easily, like a man, then she looked down at him, and there were tears in her eyes and she was like a woman. He went to the stable and asked for his mount. To the stableman he said, "Any news about the judge?"

"He's bad hurt, but the doc thinks he'll pull through."

Ross swung into the saddle, and together he and Lenore Warrington rode down Bridge Street toward where the Saboba road made off across the plains and the river trail branched west and south to the XR headquarters. In front of Fransen's they saw Don Diego Palomar. The little Mexican turned his head as if he did not want to see them.

They rode across the bridge; to the left were the long, makeshift warehouses where the barbed wire for the XR fence was stored. There were a half-dozen idle wagons that had been used recently for hauling posts, and in a corral beyond that were twenty mules.

And suddenly it was more than a fence. It was money and sweating men and torn flesh; back-breaking labor under a merciless sun. It was progress and accomplishment, and beyond that it was fighting and misunderstanding and bloodshed. He thought of the money that was there in his shirt front and he thought of the contractors who had failed in putting through that north-line fence that could have been the means of fencing off a war. He knew then that he could not drift on as he had done before; he would have to be a part of things. It was strong in him, and it was the same drive that had made him a saddle tramp, only now it was driving him to stay. He looked at Lenore, and he saw that she was staring straight ahead, her face set.

Then, unbidden, as it always came, was the picture of Jean Hedley. The nights when the stars had been close to the earth; the days she had ridden with him and talked of nothing. The touch of her hand when they had said good-by here at the edge of Saboba. And tonight the softness of her body, the horrible crying out of her need for protection and help; the surging sting of her grief that would be worse now that her mother was gone. There was a choking lump in his throat.

They rode fast, and in the scent of the new grass and the touch of the wind he still found a part of Jean Hedley and he wondered why this should be so.

13

IT WAS NEAR where the river bore sharply north to cross the south line of Ed Tozier's place that they saw the camp fire and came upon the posse disconsolately squatting on their heels, arguing among themselves. Sellew was there, and the men he had brought with him from town. And across the rim of firelight Ross saw Gib Baudry, a massive, misshapen hulk in a battered and stained blanket coat. A couple of XR men that Ross hadn't noticed before were matching notes with the sheriff.

Tony came out and held Lenore's horse while she dismounted and for a second they were close together in the half-light outside the fire glow. Ross heard Sellew say, "You can't keep it up forever, kid. You better think over what I've been telling you." He could see Tony put his arm around Lenore's waist and pull her close to him. He couldn't tell for sure whether Sellew kissed her or not. He felt a hard knot in the pit of his stomach and he thought of Queenie back there in Ben Fransen's saloon.

Sheriff Bill Yates, a colorless man with a pessimistic way about him, said, "We didn't find that Hedley kid but we found out where you're short another hundred head of steers, Miss Lenore."

Lenore was standing close to Ross now, her arm touching his. A few feet away Tony Sellew had a twisted grin on his lips and a laugh in his eyes. He kept looking straight at Lenore.

One of the XR men Ross didn't know said, "It's that hundred head we had cut out in that meadow just north of Cache Creek, Miss Lenore." They still called her that.

"Me and Fen was up at the line shack. We was gonna make a swing south like you said."

She kept staring at the fire, saying nothing. Her shoulders drooped some, and the rough clothing she wore was oddly in conflict with the almost helpless femininity of her face. It was the way the fire glow fell, Ross told himself. It was fatigue.

And yet it was something more than that, he knew. The thought kept persisting that here was a girl he had never known, even though he had once thought he loved her. But by what standard can a man judge love? It was a country of few women and he had been young and full of dreams. And now it was a pitch-dark night and there was a posse of men bent on killing another man. There was a fire that threw deep, chiseled shadows across hard faces. Talk of wholesale rustling; a hundred head of beef. The taint of war along a devil's fenceline. And yet he thought of her, and for the first time he thought of her not as a woman to heap fuel on his long-banked passion but as a woman completely alone. A woman who needed a friend.

The sheriff was saying, "What fence there is built there along Murdock's ain't doin no good. They went around it, just as they always do. They drove the stock right across Murdock's place this time, but they're still headin' for the railroad. Left a trail as wide as a county road. I'm takin' a few of the boys here with me to follow it up, but I don't reckon it's gonna do much good. Can't tell but what the Hedley kid was in with 'em and took the cattle train."

The men got up, splitting into two groups now, those who were going to return to Saboba and those few who had decided to stick with the sheriff to follow the obvious trail of the stolen herd. Sellew touched Ross on the arm with the side of his hand, said, "Thanks for riding out with Lenore. See you later."

There was a certin cocksureness in the way he said it—
a possessiveness Ross didn't like. But it was not his place
to argue the personal affairs of Lenore Warrington, so
he said nothing. Lenore turned quickly, a sharp decisive-
ness in her voice. "You take a couple of our men and go
with the sheriff, Tony. Report back to me at the ranch
as soon as you know anything."

It was a flat order, as completely final as old Tuck
Brant himself would have given it. Sellew colored slightly,
shrugged his shoulders, and walked over to his horse.
Most of the men had mounted. Lenore gave her orders
to the rest of the crew. "Riggs, you and Fen get on back
to the line shack and go on with your checking of that
south quarter. Tilman, Benson, go with Sellew."

As suddenly as it had left her she was again the owner
of the XR, and yet in her orders there was something
more than command. It was almost as if she were trying
now to take the sharp sting out of the order she had given
Sellew.

Tony had mounted and ridden his horse close. He sat
there a minute, the horse fretting, and he looked down at
Lenore. There was the same sureness in his eyes that Ross
had noticed when Tony had ordered Queenie to sing that
song. There was a half-smile on his handsome face. He
reached down quickly and pinched Lenore on the cheek.
"See you later, sweetheart," he said. He wheeled his horse,
sank the spurs, and was into the darkness.

Ross saw the whiteness that was more fear than anger
on Lenore's face. He took her arm, saying, "Come on,
Lenore. I'll ride on in with you."

They rode down the trail toward where the XR headquarters set deep in the rolling land on the east bank of
the Sasinaw. And, in time, the sprawling layout was there
below them, and Ross felt that quick catch of breath that
he had felt a dozen times before when he looked down on
the citadel of Tuck Brant.

The buildings of the XR were dull and formless in the murky half-light of near morning, but even that murkiness could not erase the formidable lines of this giant of the plains. For Tuck Brant had been a man of huge proportions, both physically and in his way of doing things, and his hand was keenly visible in the barn, the corrals, the bunkhouse, and especially on the headquarters ranch house itself.

There was no flamboyant cry of wealth about the architecture. Rather there was a massive, immobile solidness about it that said it was here to stay. There was something about it that reminded a man of the towering escarpment that sliced off the east edge of the high plain.

In the days when Tuck Brant had first come here, Indians had not yet been herded onto reservations, and the United States Cavalry did not ride to the bugle-blaring rescue of one man. A short way to the south and west *comancheros* still traded with Apaches; traded supplies stolen from ranchers and others not big enough to resist.

So Tuck Brant had decided to be big enough to last, and had made his buildings flaunting banners to that decision. The main house itself was built of adobe blocks, blocks three feet thick on the outer walls. At first there had been gun slits that had served as windows; some of them were still visible in the square structure that had been the first room. Later the house had grown, and now there was a long porch with a brick floor and heavy arches supporting hand-hewn beams brought three hundred miles by muleback.

As Tuck Brant and his holdings grew, he took a wife, and later there was a daughter. The square house with its porch became an "L," and after that a "U," with its block center section and its two wings. Between these wings, so Ross had heard, a flower garden had once grown, but when Tuck's wife died the flowers died, too, and had never been replanted. Women in town said it had been more than the loneliness of the plains and the drive of Tuck Brant that had killed his wife. Women in town said it was the heartbreak of seeing him hate a daughter when he wanted a son.

So now, where there had been flowers there was the hard-tramped earth where ready horses sometimes stood before well-gnawed hitch rails. This morning those rails were empty: the house was alone and desolate—dark, silent, and unyielding, as it had always been. The house of a cattle king; the house of that man's daughter. They dismounted there in the courtyard, and she opened the door that was never locked. He waited a minute, not sure; then she said, "Come on inside, Ross."

The headquarters sat on the top of an imperceptible knoll, and behind it, two hundred yards or more, was the slow-moving Sasinaw. In front was the endless range of the XR, undulating with grass and distance, unbroken except for the summer-dry arroyo of Coyote Creek and the dusty ruts of the Saboba road; on, then, across the nothingness of grass, into the breaks of the Catclaw, beyond that, even, to the escarpment itself. A range so vast that no human eye could see the end of it. But here Tuck Brant had set, and in his mind he could touch each corner of his domain and count the cattle that roamed unchecked by fence or neighbor.

Here he had raised his daughter, and always he had wanted a son. He had sent her to school, and in his way he had made her a lady, but always he had remained firm in his belief that her real heritage was this land. She could buy her help and rule her kingdom, and if there was a place in her life for love, he never admitted it.

These things Ross knew, and he felt them as he stood there in the massive doorway under the long, arched porch. He could feel the leaden press of the sky, the morning cut of the air. The door of the long bunkhouse opened, and a man threw out a pan of water, then the door closed again, and there was new smoke from the bunkhouse chimney.

They went into the dungeonlike front room, thick with the echoes of their footsteps, and there was more than the coldness of the night seeping from the cavernous fireplace, flanked by its unbelievable steer-horn chairs and a massive, hand-carved bench, rigid with uncomfortableness. The one piece of elegance in the room was a lion-footed mahogany table that would have been oversize in a room twice as gigantic as this.

Lenore turned up the lamp that was burning low there on the table, and she motioned Ross to follow her down the dark corridor that led to the left wing of the house. The cold soullessness of the front room touched Ross and left him ill at ease, like an anticipated challenge; it was the way Tuck Brant had planned his guests should feel.

He was acutely conscious of Lenore now. A dozen times he had seen her like this—in half-boots, skin-tight blue denims, and a faded flannel shirt with a neckerchief knotted tightly around her throat. She was the owner of the XR, and wore clothes in keeping with her heritage, clothes that were made to fit the business that was so much a part of her. Someone had said once, "I don't see why Brant squalls about not having a son. He didn't miss far."

Now with the light of the lamp shining up on her face Ross again got the feeling that it was only the clothes people saw, and few had ever seen the woman who wore them. It was as if she were wearing a costume for a play, desperately anxious to win the approval of the critics, knowing all the while that she was not actress enough to carry it. She took off her battered felt hat and her hair was soft, with a well-groomed sheen about it. It tumbled loosely down the back of her neck, and he saw that it was caught back with two plain silver clasps.

When she removed her heavy sheepskin coat he could see the mature swell of her breasts and the creamy whiteness of her throat, a whiteness that had been adamant against the land and the weather. She moved gracefully, and yet ill at ease. What light there was caught in the prisms of her eyes as she turned and knocked on the door there near the end of the hall. Tall, willowy, supremely confident with her heritage, strangely lost in her role. She nodded her head back toward the big living room and said, "Herbert and I never use that part of the house."

The door on which she had knocked opened a crack and a Chinaman as old as the XR itself showed part of his bland face. The steaming smell of the kitchen came into the hall, the rich headiness of good food and fresh coffee. It hung there like a curtain. Lenore said, "Is Mr. Warrington awake yet, Chang?"

Chang said, "Not know. He not here. Chang busy." He closed the door.

It seemed to bother her. Ross saw her bite her lower lip quickly and she hesitated, her hand on the doorknob of the door across the hall from the kitchen. Then she shrugged her shoulders as if it didn't matter much, but in the movement Ross saw that it actually did matter. More than she cared to admit. She said, "Come on in."

She opened the door and he walked out of the cold austerity of Tuck Brant's past into a different world. And somehow he felt it was the world of Herbert Warrington, not of Lenore Brant.

What once had been three rooms had been made into one. A long, low, glass-paned window looked out across the prairie, the picture framed on one side by a lane of cottonwood. There was huge-flowered wallpaper, gaudy in its way, yet subtle and rich. The long window seat was piled deep with cushions, and stretched there like an invitation to good living. A fire burned brightly in a large fireplace that had a carved beam for a mantel. There was a ship model there, and there was deep pile carpeting on the floor. The furniture was rich hand-rubbed mahogany that had an obvious delicacy about it, yet gave the impression of permanence. It was like the delicacy Ross had noticed in Herbert Warrington.

She took the hat he still held awkwardly in his hand and motioned him toward a leather-covered chair. "I'll have Chang get us some breakfast," she said. "I imagine Herbert will be back in a little while. He likes to ride early in the morning." He got the feeling she had made that up quickly.

She excused herself and went into another room, and in the second the door was open Ross caught sight of a massive mahogany bed and chintz-covered chairs. The door closed, and he was alone there with his thoughts, completely ill at ease.

The affairs of the night piled in on him then. The fight there at Fransen's; the guilt of Bret Hedley; the death of Maw. And overshadowing all his thoughts was the frightening blank stare he had seen in the eyes of Jean. A complete hopelessness that had been etched into her features as she stood there in the middle of the street, calling her brother's name.

His full hatred turned again to Ben Fransen, and he began trying to piece things together, trying to connect Fransen with every bit of trouble that had happened here along the Sasinaw. And he wondered, too, about Tony Sellew, and the disgust that had been in Herbert Warrington's voice, and of the quick intimacy he had seen between the XR foreman and Lenore. But, most of all, as he looked around the room, he thought of Herbert Warrington himself, and he came to know him by the room itself. A strange man. There was comfort and beauty in this room, but there was more than that. There was a raw, nerve-shattering conflict, the conflict of a man trying to be recognized for himself alone in a place that accepted nothing less than a Brant.

He didn't hear the door open. He wasn't aware that she was standing there until he turned and saw her. She had put on an expensive wrapper, belted around the waist, and her half-boots had been replaced by fussy slippers. She had a single sheet of note paper in her hand and she kept staring straight ahead, just as Jean Hedley had stared straight ahead when Ross had held her there in front of Ben Fransen's. Her face was dead white.

He got up quickly, startled by the expression on her face and the total silence of the room. He called her name, and she started toward him, walking slowly, dazed. He thought she might fall, and he put out his arms. She pushed them down, as if accepting help would be outside her code. She spoke slowly, deliberately, not to him, not to anyone. "He's left me, Ross. I didn't believe he would, but he's left me."

14

FOR A MOMENT there was that strange uneasiness that comes to a man alone with a woman. He was afraid she would cry and he was afraid she wouldn't. He was completely helpless in the face of the situation.

Once he had asked himself what difference it would make if Herbert Warrington were to leave her; now he was anxious to console her. He knew that in this second she was horribly alone and he wanted to help her and he didn't know how.

She went to the sofa in front of the fireplace, sat down, and gripped her hands together, holding them in her lap. She said softly, "Come sit by me, Ross."

He sat down by her awkwardly, and said the first useless and senseless thing that came to his mind. "I wouldn't get all worked up over it."

She was staring straight ahead into the fire. She said, "Just sit there, Ross. Don't say anything. Don't even listen if you don't want to. Just let me talk. I've got to talk."

He felt a cold chill in every nerve of his body. Seeing her like this was like watching the kingdom of Tuck Brant tumble; it was like seeing the XR cut up into tiny farm plots; it was like seeing a man lose the work of a lifetime. And then he saw it in the widening of her eyes, the helpless droop of her full lips, the strain that was etching lines into her face. It was the same thing he had seen in the face of Jean Hedley—the face of a woman losing someone she loves. He said, "I didn't know before how you felt about him, Lenore."

He took her hands then and held them and she didn't look at him. She said simply, "I gambled and lost, Ross. I thought I could whip everything that got in my way. I was raised to think that way."

The mood of her touched him, and he spoke without knowing what he was saying. Spoke words that perhaps had come to his mind in dreams under star-heavy skies. He said, "You're young yet and beautiful. It's not as if another man couldn't love you."

She said, "There's whisky there in that commode. Will you pour me a drink?"

He got up, his hands trembling when he took the bottle and the two glasses. He poured each glass nearly full. She sat there, turning the glass in her hand, and after a while she sipped the liquor, sipped it as if she couldn't taste it. She said softly, "I hated my father, Ross. I hated everything he stood for."

He knew that he couldn't interrupt, couldn't reason. He downed his drink and poured himself another, and slowly the tears came to Lenore Brant Warrington's eyes and rolled down her cheeks. She didn't try to brush ther away. "I've tried to be what he made me," she said then. "And God knows why I tried except that I wanted to show him he was wrong. He said once that if Mother had died bearing him a son it would have been worth it. He said she died for nothing."

There was no sob in her voice, no hysterical weeping. Just the dry, tearing collapse of the role she had played so long—the role she had not been able to fill.

"If I had been tall and rawboned and ugly—I would have cut my hair short and learned to handle a gun and maybe I would have killed a man——"

"Don't, Lenore." She sipped at the whisky and ignored his interruptions.

"But I was a woman, and I've always been a woman, and I did crazy things to men's minds, even when I was trying to be their equal. I tried to ride horses the way you rode them, Ross. You were closer to my age than anyone here. I tried to be like you, and even you didn't understand."

"I was in love with you." His voice was husky and unnatural.

"You never were." She said it quickly, viciously. "I know how you felt, because I was caught in the same trap myself. You wanted me, yes, but you never loved me. You were burning up inside, crazy. Crazy enough to kill a man who did nothing more wrong than admitting the things you yourself felt. That's not love, Ross. It's man and woman. I've seen it in the eyes of a dozen men who have never even spoken to me. It gets to be a disgusting thing to watch, and when I was tired of it I tried harder than ever to be Tuck Brant's son. And then I was caught by the same thing, and I know what I'm talking about."

His heart was thudding hard, high in his chest. His throat felt dry and his tongue swollen. He said thickly, "Tony Sellew?"

She turned toward him for the first time, and he tried to avoid her eyes. "Yes, Tony Sellew," she said. "I tried being a woman. All the woman that had been held back by jeans and boots, and a father who wanted a son. When he glanced at me the first time I knew I had to be a woman—just once. When he touched my hand I wanted him so completely that I was unable to think of anything else." She drained the glass, and as naturally as a man might toss away a cigarette she threw the glass into the fireplace.

He wanted to stop her—didn't want to hear the rest of it. Yet he couldn't say a word.

"Tony was smart," she said bitterly. "He let me wait, and with every minute of waiting it became torture, and he waited until I went crawling on my hands and knees to him, begging him for favors." She stopped, and he could hear her shallow breathing, see the flare of her nostrils, the hard set of her lips. She said, "And then it was over, and I felt cheap and unclean and the thing I had called love was gone and in its place there was nothing but disgust. I promised myself then I'd make him pay for it the rest of his life."

"And now Sellew threatens to tell Warrington?" It was the first direct question he had asked her.

"He doesn't have to threaten," she said. "He has a way of looking at a man and putting all the filth there is into that look. He thinks that once he's had a woman she'll never be able to forget him. He says that someday I'll leave Herbert and come crawling back to him and it's there in his eyes every time he looks at Herbert."

His heartbeats were slower now, his breathing more normal. In the minutes it had taken her to tell it he had relived every agonizing moment of his own desires, his own feelings toward her. It was the thing he had called his love. And in reliving it he came to recognize it for what it was and now it was gone, completely dead, and now that he saw it, it could never be dangerous again. He could look at her as he might look at any other woman who needed help. He said, "You should have fired him, Lenore. Why didn't you?"

She seemed to have better control of herself now. She said, "Because I'm a Brant. It would have been admitting he had whipped me. It's the same thing that made me gamble on trying to be a man when I ran the XR and a woman when I loved my husband. I've been taught to back down from nothing, Ross, not even my emotions. It's the only way of living I know." He let her talk, knowing it was what she needed.

She said, "It was perfect at first, Herbert and I. I was actually a woman for the first time in my life. Dad hated it, and in watching his hate I knew I had whipped him. And then Dad was killed and every place I looked there was Dan Murdock and Diego Palomar and Ed Tozier and Gib Baudry and Loop Fenton, and they were all so smug and satisfied, and they looked at me as if they knew they had me whipped. And then I didn't care if that north fence was ever finished, and I said so. I tried to buy up their mortgages from Fransen, and I doubled the guards along the river, and told them to string up the first man they found touching one of my cows."

"And they got Loop Fenton."

"It made me sick, Ross," she said softly. "Just like Tony Sellew made me sick. I wasn't cut out to murder any more than I was to love more than one man. It isn't those men north of the river who are stealing my stock. I knew it then and I know it now. That's why I was willing to ride in with Baudry and Palomar yesterday afternoon. I was trying to make up for my mistake. Herbert wouldn't believe me. He thought I wanted to fight."

"Who do you figure is heading the rustling, Lenore?" He asked it hopefully.

She said, "I don't know."

"Ben Fransen?" Ross said. There was a cold steadiness about him such as he had felt when he had gone to Ben Fransen's room above the saloon.

"If it is, there's no way to prove it," she said. "Tony hates Fransen. He's tried to catch him in one slip. There haven't been any."

He would have liked to have gone on with it, figured out a way to prove it, but they heard the sound of the horses and the talking of the men out by the corrals and the complaint of saddles. She went to the window and said, "It's the sheriff and Sellew. They're back."

They heard the pound of boots on the front porch, and then the rapping on the foot-thick door. Chang left the whisper of padding feet as he went to the hall to let them into the big living room. She dried her eyes and looked at Ross, and there was an embarrassed little smile on her lips that made her seem younger than she was. She reached out and took his hand quickly, and said simply, "Thanks, Ross. Thanks a lot."

And then she was herself again. As much as she would ever be herself—the owner of the XR. She went down the hall, into the cavernous living room with its cold fireplace and its steer-horn chairs. She didn't ask the men to sit down. Standing there in the doorway, she spoke much as Tuck Brant himself might have spoken. One word, "Well?"

"We followed the trail plumb up to the railroad, Miss Lenore," the sheriff said. "There wasn't no sign of nothin'. Them rustlers know what they're doin', I tell you. They got cars all ready on the sidin' and arrangements all made with the railroad. The damn railroad—excuse me, ma'am—don't care what kind of cows they haul, just so they get paid for haulin' 'em."

"There's a station agent there," she said quickly. "Didn't he know anything?"

The sheriff shrugged helplessly. "Said there was five

men in the crew. Only saw one of 'em to talk to. Big jigger, flat in the face, sort of a dimple like in his chin, kinda beady-eyed, he said. That there don't mean nothin'. Fifty fellers hereabouts look like that."

"Trip Levitt," Ross thought. He knew it as surely as he was standing here. Trip Levitt. He said only, "Any line on young Hedley?"

The sheriff said, "How you gonna tell? Feller there at the station said one young buck went along with the cattle cars. Might have been Hedley—maybe it wasn't. You ain't got nothin' to go on. No more than we had before." The sheriff rolled a cud of tobacco to the side of his mouth and said, "Speakin' unofficial like, now, I'd say as long as there's open line between you and your neighbors to the north there's gonna be trouble. I ain't accusin' nobody nor mentionin' no names and I ain't free to say all I know, but it's dern funny to me them cows always take out across the Murdock place or the Palomar place or the Tozier place."

Ross said heatedly, "Where the hell do you expect them to go to get to the railroad? Down the main street of Saboba?"

The sheriff shrugged again. He said, "I was just speakin' unofficial like, as the feller says. If I knowed who was doin' it I'd arrest 'em, wouldn't I? All's I say is there ain't gonna be no stop to it unless the XR or somebody else moves out of the country. Either that or get a four-strand bob-wire fence along that north line, and I don't reckon you're gonna do that."

"Why not?" Ross asked it coldly, flatly.

"Because you ain't gonna get no more contractors to take the job, that's why not," the sheriff said. "Hell, there's been six men killed tryin' to dig postholes along that line. They got in about twenty-two miles of fence, and it's been cut twenty-two times. I talked to the contractor you had up there this time. He walked off the job flat, and he says there ain't enough money in the country to get him to go back on it. I tell you there ain't nobody fool enough to try to build that fence, so if you want to head off trouble you gotta do it another way. I'm just talkin' to you now as an old friend of your dad, Miss Lenore. I ain't talkin' to you official."

Ross turned to Lenore, looked at her steadily a long time, and then said slowly. "I want the truth, Lenore. Do you want that fence along the north line or don't you?"

She held his gaze, her eyes still red, her face still strained and pale. And in her eyes he saw that stark, hopeless love for the husband she hadn't been able to hold and he saw the murderous hell of her fight against herself and against Tony Sellew and against the thing her father had tried to make her—all this battling against the woman she had been born to be. He knew her now better than he had ever known her in his life, better perhaps than any other man had ever known her, and he knew that she realized the only way she could ever win a life of her own would be to have peace along the Sasinaw. He didn't even wait for her answer. He said, "All right, Lenore. Draw up the papers and I'll see that that fence goes through."

The sheriff scoffed loudly and snorted through his mustache. He said, "That's mighty high-soundin' talk fer a feller like you, Parnell. Just who you figger on gettin' to build that fence?"

"Myself," Ross said softly. He touched his right thumb against his chest. "Me."

15

THE SHERIFF was a blunt man who lacked the dignity of diplomacy and the ability to cover surprise. He blustered

some, and had more to say about big talk and damn fool-
ishness, until Ross, tired of it, said, "What's the matter,
Sheriff? Don't you want to see that north fence go in?"

The sheriff stood there, batting his puffy eyes, blowing
through his mustache. "I'm a law-enforcement officer,"
he blustered. "It's none of my damn affair what you do."

"Then keep it that way," Ross said. "If I break a law
I'll call on you."

The sheriff had no answer. He turned and stalked out
of the room, and in a while they heard him calling to his
men and through one of the front windows they could
see him riding back to Saboba, thickset, sloppy in the
saddle, puffed with his own importance.

Tony Sellew started to follow Ross and Lenore back
to the main living section of the house, and Lenore said,
"I'll handle this, Tony. Get Ross a riding horse and give
him a couple of men who have had some experience on
that south fence. He'll have trouble enough getting himself a crew."

Sellew shrugged. He said, "Your funeral, Parnell." He
turned and went outside.

Ross watched him go, a feeling more of acute annoyance than dislike in him. He said, "You're playing it
wrong, Lenore. Get rid of him." She didn't answer.

She had a copy of the contract papers there in Herbert
Warrington's desk and it was simple enough. It called for
a payment of one hundred fifty dollars a mile for a fence
to be laid out over a pre-surveyed course, total payment
to be made upon satisfactory completion of the fence:
the fence to be four strands of Glidden barbed wire or
equivalent, with posts no more than forty feet apart, with
sufficient wire stays to assure rigidity, and with bracing
at any point where the fence made a corner. At the crossing of the Sassinaw the fence was to extend into the
water at least ten feet from each bank, figuring the water
at summer level. The contract also called for the posting

of a one-thousand-dollar good-faith bond. When Ross's finger had traced that far on the paper Lenore said, "You can forget that part of it, Ross." Then nervously, "I know you were only trying to help, Ross. You don't have to go through with it."

He looked at her and he grinned, a wide, easy-going, boyish grin. He said, "Look, kid. I been running away from things for a long time, including you. I'm a little tired of it." He reached into his shirt front and took out the packet of bills and laid it on the desk in front of him. He said, "It's the first time I've ever had a chance to swing a deal on my own." There was a touch of cockiness in his voice.

She asked him about the money, not prying, and he told her briefly about his run of luck at Ben Fransen's. There was enough of Tuck Brant about her to make her like the possible irony of the situation. She said, "You wouldn't use a man's own money to choke him with, would you, Ross?"

He said, "I would, and I'd like it." He scrawled his signature on the bottom of the contract.

She shook hands with him and for a while he stood there, holding her hand, and then he reached out and gripped her by the shoulder. He said, "Someday when I get a chance I'm gonna have a talk with that husband of yours."

He thought he saw a slight glisten of tears in her eyes. She said, "I won't tell you not to."

He crooked his finger under her chin and pushed it upward. "Keep it there," he said. "And meanwhile, wear a dress."

She said, "Thanks, Ross." And she meant it.

He went out to the corrals, and he sucked the bite of morning air into his lungs and found a new life in his step, a new strength in his muscles. He knew now, without being told, that the same drive that made a man a drifter could make him a winner. He knew nothing about building a fence, and until he had seen that south fence there with the Hedleys, wire had meant nothing in his life. But there had been something about the magnitude of that project that had stirred the imagination in him and touched an ambition that he had been trying to keep dormant. At this moment he had more money than he had ever possessed in his life; once he would have used it as a way to make drifting a career. But now he wanted to risk it on a proposition that would make him keep his feet planted in one spot. In doing it he was going to bring someone out in the open and force a showdown, and out of the things that happened he hoped that Herbert Warrington would be able to see his wife as clearly as Ross had seen her this morning.

He came around the corner of the barn and saw two men already mounted; he saw Sellew standing there holding the bridle of a huge, clean-limbed grulla dun with the bold XR burned on its left hip. Sellew jerked his head toward the mounted men and said, "Page and Farrel. They've built fence before and they'll tell you what they know. I'll need them back in a week." Ross recognized them as two of the men who had ridden with Trip Levitt that day where the south fence blocked off the Saboba road.

Ross said, "I want to see you a minute, Sellew. Alone."

They went inside the barn and Sellew stood there, making a cigarette, his eyes never leaving Ross's face. He was a tall, sinewy man, as tall as Ross, and heavier built, and his hands, graceful and slim, were large enough to be effective as fists. But the thing that stuck in a man's mind was the handsomeness of Sellew's face, the perfection of features, the taunting curve of his lips, the haunting enigma that was always in his eyes. He licked the cigarette and said, "What's on your mind, Parnell?"

"Lenore," Ross said softly. "I don't want to hear of you bothering her again."

Sellew showed no flicker of emotion. He said, "Suppose you let her handle her own affairs."

"I'm telling you again: leave her alone."

"And if I don't?"

"I'll beat hell out of you."

Tony snapped his nail against the match head and lit his cigarette. He inhaled deeply and blew the sheet of smoke through tightly compressed lips. He said, "It's been tried before, Parnell."

"Not by me," Ross said. "Leave her alone."

He turned, went back, and mounted the grulla dun, noting that it was his own saddle they had put on the animal. Motioning to Page and Farrel, he rode out of the corral and turned toward the river trail that led back to the breaks where six months' time and three contractors had netted a total of twenty-two miles of fence. He half-turned in his saddle and said, "I want to look over the setup. You been up there?"

Page said, "Should we have been?" He would get little or no help here, he saw.

Farrel said, "We'll tell you what we know about building a fence. Ask questions along that line and you'll get answers."

Ross took it and said nothing. He was in business now. In business to build a hundred miles of fence at a hundred and fifty dollars a mile. A five-thousand-dollar profit on an original ten-thousand-dollar investment—a lot of money. Enough money that a man could afford to keep his temper reined close and his eyes and ears open.

They kept left where Cache Creek came into the Sasinaw and crossed at the gravelly ford. The water was belly-high on the horses in the new spring runoff. Beyond this the country became a series of deep-gash gullies with straight, red clay sides, sheer drops of a hundred feet or more. The bottoms of these twisting canyons were dense with cottonwood, and in some places the ground was boggy and soft. It was a strip of eroded country that ran between the river and the unfenced lines of the ranches to the north, and, stretching down the middle of it in a nearly straight line, was a flat, low-lying table-land formation a mile or more wide. It was down the middle of this flat, floored canyon that Ross Parnell was to build his fence.

West again then, and from his memory of having worked these breaks in spring roundup when he rode as an XR hand, Ross knew they were skirting the line of Don Diego's Rancho Los Lobos, and a few miles on he knew they were on Dan Murdock's range.

The ground flattened away some, and there were cattle, wild as deer, that hit the brush ahead of them. Don Diego's Stirrup brand; the big-as-a-barnside brand of the XR; Dan Murdock's walking M, and even a few of old Ed Tozier's T Cross stuff. All together here in the breaks, and during the spring roundup it was not strange that sometimes a man might brand the wrong calf. It had always been that way, and always Tuck Brant had bellowed and yelled himself hoarse, admitting he could lose a thousand calves and not miss 'em, but damned if he'd put up with the principle of the thing.

And then they came to the obvious hoof-lashed trail where a hundred head of cattle had been driven north, and Ross knew that this was no branding of strays, no neighborly mavericking of an XR table yearling. This was full-scale wholesale rustling. Thought out, well executed, and foolproof. As he thought of that, he again thought of Ben Fransen, and he knew that he wasn't too far wrong.

Someday someone would make a slip. And then it wouldn't be a matter of guesswork any more. But, for the time being, a fence along this line was the first step in the right direction, for it would come closer than anything else to smothering out the war that was brewing between the XR and its neighbors.

He tried to convince himself that it wasn't only the thing that had happened to Bret Hedley that had built this sudden hatred for Ben Fransen. Bret's trouble, he told himself, had merely been the thing that had let him see it clearly; the fuse that had set off the cap. The rest of the men around Saboba had been too close to the picture; it had come on them too gradually. As an outsider he had been able to view it all with an objectivity that was impossible for men like Dan Murdock and Diego Palomar. Farrel interrupted his thoughts. He said, "Looks like yonder is your baby, Parnell."

They rode up to a wagon that was turned over on its side—a scatter of posts, and a few spools of snarled wire. There were two rows of stakes where a tent had been set on high ground, a cleared circle and a pile of blackened stones where the camp fire had burned. Beyond that wagon ruts followed a line of set posts to which the wire had not been attached, and farther was the twenty-two miles of completed fence.

Ross got down and surveyed the setup, not knowing for sure what he was trying to find, knowing only that there was a thrill in him now that drifting had never been able to give him. The wire and the posts held as much fascination for him as cards or roulette once had. It was the same feel, the gamble of being right or wrong. He could picture the fence, splitting the center of this long, flat canyon, strong and unyielding, silver bars against the white and blue of the summer skies, solidly untouchable in the grip of winter. Out of the canyon and down the slope into the valley, across the Sasinaw, across the plains south of Saboba, and on to the Catclaw. A man-made barrier as effective as the barrier of the escarpment. And Herbert Warrington would plant wheat east of the Catclaw, he knew, and another fence would corner this one and bear south to meet the drift fence that cut the high plains. And the XR would be an empire of grass and cows, an empire even of wheat, completely enclosed by barbed wire.

He talked of posts and staples and stretching of wire, and he got short answers from the men Sellew had sent to help him. Cedar posts he would have to haul over fifty miles; cottonwood was there in the bottom of the breaks, if he could find a way to snake it out. He'd use cedar only in the boggy spots, he decided.

Kicking around at the water-soaked ashes of the camp fire, Ross said, "Don't look like there's been any work here for a month. Who was it had that contract?"

"Feller name of Swensen," Farrel said. "Done a lot of big fencin' in the Panhandle—XIT, LE's. Come in with more equipment than you could shake a stick at, but I reckon he figgered it was cheaper to forfeit his bond than try to finish this one."

"Know where I can find him?" Ross asked.

"Town, I reckon. Don't see him here, do you?"

"Wanta come along and have a drink?"

Farrel shrugged and looked at Page. "Why not?"

They rode back and forded the Sasinaw in the approximate spot where the fence would cross it, then headed on for Saboba, getting there about one in the afternoon. When they skirted the Tozier place Ross thought of old Sam Hedley and of Bret and Maw, but mostly he thought of Jean. He wondered if it was possible that Bret had made his escape and caught the cattle train, and there was a strange conflict of emotions as he thought of Judge Iverson, shot down in the street, and then thought of the complete, whipped misery he had seen on the face of Jean. He said nothing to the two men Sellew had loaned him.

Saboba was quiet after its close brush with death, and when they crossed the bridge there were not more than a half-dozen horses at the hitch racks there in the main street. Ross took another look at the long, temporary warehouse and for the first time noticed the sign, SWENSEN CONSTRUCTION COMPANY. He said, "Reckon that's as good a place to try as any."

He turned his horse and rode down the wagon road into the long, flat yard where bales of wire were piled and the empty post wagons stood in rows, on past the corral with its twenty or more mules, and then to the little shack marked "Office," with its sign: MEN WANTED. He dismounted and went inside. He saw an old codger, half-asleep, with his feet on the desk. Ross said, "You work for Swensen?"

The old man looked at him thoughtfully, took his feet off the desk and said, "Ten year now. If you're lookin' fer a job you're too late. Swensen pulled out early this morning to take a job up north of the railroad. Got all the men he needs up there."

Ross said, "Then why don't you take down the sign?"

The old man said, "Ain't got around to it."

Ross went to the single square window, rubbed off the dust with his elbow, and looked out at the equipment. He looked over his shoulder, jerked his thumb toward the yard with its stockpile of wire and its row of wagons. He said, Swensen leaving this stuff here?"

"It's there, ain't it?" the old man said.

"Would he be interested in selling it?"

The old man spit on the floor and said, "You ask a heap of questions."

"I'm interested in buying it," Ross said.

The old man rolled his tongue against the inside of his lower lip, spit, and said, "See Ben Fransen then. It's him as owns it. He bought it up not over two hour ago."

16

Ross DIDN'T waste his time arguing with the old man. He went back outside and found that his two helpers had already left, more interested in getting a drink than in whether or not Ross got wagons and wire and mules. He mounted the XR grulla and rode up the nearly deserted street.

His idea was to go first and see how Judge Iverson was making out, but the horses and the buggy in front of Ben Fransen's saloon changed his mind. He recognized the white-stockinged bay that Dan Murdock always rode and the buggy belonged to Diego Palomar. He felt a strange twist of apprehension, and he reined in, dismounted, and tied his horse to the hitch rail.

From inside he could hear the haranguing voice of Ben Fransen. It sounded as if the man was making an election speech. Ross pushed open the doors and went inside.

Fransen was on the small stage, emphasizing his words with a flailing fist. Standing in front of him in a shoulder-to-shoulder semi-circle were Murdock and Palomar and Gib Baudry, flanked by a half-dozen toughs Ross remembered having seen before in Hogtown. Page and Farrel were standing at the far end of the bar having a drink. They were paying no attention to Ben Fransen.

Fransen had stepped completely out of his casual, half-arrogant air and was carrying on like a politician. Ross heard him say, "It's not the first time Sheriff Bill Yates has let us down. I still say it's not the fault of the man. He's got too much territory to cover. But I say we've got a right to demand that he keep up the search. This Hedley is a murderer. Whether he's working alone or working for the XR we don't know, but he has killed a man who was our friend."

"I haven't the men to spare," Diego Palomar argued.

"You know damn well I can't take the time, Ben." Dan Murdock said.

"So we've got these men here," Fransen said, sweeping his hand toward the Hogtown crew. "When I've got a job to do I hire men to do it; this is no different. Arm these men, deputize them, give them the single job of finding Hedley, and back them up!"

Gib Baudry, parrotlike, said, "Sounds like the way to do it."

"Will the sheriff go along with the idea?" Dan Murdock wanted to know.

Ross walked up in back of the men, his drink still in his hand. He said, "Why the sudden public spirit, Ben?"

There was a quick, flat silence. Diego Palomar moved aside slightly and the prospective posse from Hogtown shifted its weight, not knowing what they were expected to do. Gib Baudry glared, but didn't move. Ben Fransen slipped quickly back into his soft, easy deadliness. He said, "We haven't forgotten you brought the Hedleys here, Parnell."

"And I had planned to leave it at that," Ross said. He turned directly to Murdock and Palomar, ignoring Baudry. "Thought you might want to know I took the contract to build that north fence you've been wanting." He downed his drink and tossed the glass in his hand. At this moment he was as supremely sure of himself as he had ever been in his life. He said, "Figured that would be news to you two; reckon it's not to Ben because he's started buying equipment out from under me already. I came to find out why, Ben."

Except for two slight lines at the corners of Ben Fransen's mouth there was no expression on his face. He waited until the touch of silence was exactly right and then he said softly, "I bought it because we want a fence, not just some more cover-up posthole digging."

"I want it plainer than that, Ben."

"All right, Parnell, you'll get it. You're XR." He was leaning forward slightly now and his right hand was gripping the edge of his coat, belt high. "You're XR, and the XR will see to it that that fence is never finished because Lenore Brant has got her heart set on grabbing more land north of the river. She came to me and tried to buy up the mortgages I hold and when I wouldn't let go she said she'd find another way. She's got that gunhawk Sellew, and she figures if there's trouble enough we'll get tired of it and make a wrong move." He waited until he knew the eyes of Palomar and Murdock were riveted to his face and then he said, "Tell me, Parnell. Can you prove that the XR doesn't drive its own cows north to the railroad on these so-called raids?"

Ross said softly, "You took your time about taking sides in this thing, Fransen."

Fransen said, "Did I? I've loaned more money than it was good sense to loan on every ranch north of the river. I haven't loaned any to the XR, have I? What's *your* record, Parnell?"

Ross looked at Diego Palomar and saw the little Mexican turn his head and busy himself with a cigarette. Murdock met his gaze levelly and held it, and there was unrelenting accusation in the eyes of the big Scot. Gib Baudry, his face still marked by Ross's fist, grinned crookedly, satisfied. He said, "You know where you stand now, Parnell."

"I do," Ross said levelly. "On my own. I'm building a fence, and I don't take orders from the XR or from you men either. If I run into trouble I'll know where to look."

He turned his back on them and left, and as he went through the doors of the saloon he thought he heard Farrel laugh shortly. It could have been at some joke Page had passed.

He had met the issue squarely, and had learned nothing, and yet he had learned everything. The complete reason for Fransen's sudden open switch to the side of the small ranchers was not apparent, but he knew it was not Fransen's fear of the XR.

He got his horse and rode up the street and over to Judge Iverson's place, and as he opened the gate and went up the walk he got that old feeling of being at home. Maria opened the door to his knock and put her arms around him and started to cry. Her crying was as much a part of her as a natural greeting is to some.

She said, "Always the judge ask for you."

He said, "How is he?"

She said, "You come look," and in the way she said it he knew the judge was all right.

He found Iverson propped up in the big bed, his left shoulder and half his chest bandaged. His face was tight and drawn but there was a lot of life in the old man's eyes and an amazing strength in his handclasp. He said, "Sit down, Ross. Tell me what's going on. I hear they haven't found young Hedley yet."

"No trace, as far as I know," said Ross. "I just came from Fransen's. He's trying to lineup a gun posse to spend full time looking for the kid."

"Sheriff Yates will probably approve that," the judge said. "He's inclined to take the easy way out."

"Fransen was selling himself to Murdock and Palomar. Seems Baudry is already sold."

"He always has been pretty thick with those three," said the judge. "He says it's because he has money tied up in their places."

"Maybe it's because their places make good blinds for what he's really up to."

"Accusing a man and proving him guilty are two different things, Ross," the judge said. "Remember that."

"Maybe I'll find out things," said Ross. "I took the contract to put through that north fence."

The judge was silent a long time, thoughtful. He kept

looking at the palm of his right hand. He said, "That's a pretty big job, Ross."

There was nothing veiled about Iverson's meaning. Ross could feel the spot of color crawling across his cheeks but there was no resentment in him. He said, "It's a big job, Judge, but I don't reckon it will be any tougher than the one I've been trying to handle for the past five years."

The judge smiled. He said simply, "I like that, Ross. As soon as a man knows where he's going he starts to get there. You'll do all right."

Ross said, "I won't get trouble from Lenore Brant. Can I count on your side?"

"You can count on us, Ross. We need that fence."

"Reckon that leaves Fransen," Ross said. "He can't be here in town and driving off XR cows at the same time so he must have help."

"Thinking of Sellew?" the judge wanted to know.

Ross shook his head. "I don't believe it. Regardless of what else Sellew is he's first a cowman. He's got ambitions, too, but they're a lot closer to home. Sellew didn't hesitate to hang Loop Fenton, did he?"

"You're right there," the judge admitted.

Ross got up and squeezed the old man's hand affectionately. "Get yourself some more rest. I'll check with you later."

"Take care of yourself, will you, boy?"

"I'll do that."

He left the room and saw Maria stooping close to the door. She put both hands on her hips and said, "So! You gonna build a fence, no?"

Ross imitated her pose and said, "So! You been listening at the door, No?"

She shrugged her massive shoulders, completely unconcerned at being caught. She said, "I gotta look out for the judge." Then, edging away from the subject, "Where you gonna get the mans to build this fence?"

Ross shook his head. The thought had perplexed him too. "I don't know," he said. "Haven't tried yet."

She said, "You know my cousin Gomez? He lives in Hogtown."

"Can't say that I do," Ross admitted.

"He's a good man." She nodded her head vigorously.

"I'll bet he is," Ross agreed.

"Three times Gomez work on that fence. Three times, poof! Trouble. He say everybody afraid to work there now."

"That's fine," Ross said. "I'll do it alone. I'll hold the post with one hand, stretch the wire with my teeth, and pound staples with my feet."

"I don't think you can do it," Maria said.

"So I'm a pelado, that it?"

"No," she said seriously. "You are not a pelado. You are my very best twin. But I think you got trouble, Ross Parnell. You go to Hogtown, and by the ditch on last end is my cousin. You tell him I say he supposed to go to work for you on fence and get some mans for you."

"All right, Maria," he promised. "If I run into trouble I'll look for Gomez. You heard anything about Mrs. Hedley?"

She nodded her head sadly, and crossed herself. "The young girl, she come to town this afternoon. I tell priest he better go out by Agnes Fenton. I think he got that girl by the church now."

"Thanks, Maria," he said, patting her arm. "I'll remember about Gomez."

He hurried out, and rode his horse the short distance to the squat, adobe building on the edge of Hogtown that was half church, half school. Hat in hand, he went inside, and was met by the somber-featured, brown-robed priest who had long ago given up trying to wipe sin from his tiny mission and now was content to do what he could for those at either extremity of the life span. Ross said, "Mrs. Hedley. I've come to see about making arrangements."

The priest said, "I'm glad you're here. There's been no one. The girl has been alone all afternoon." He led Ross to a small room, dark and dank-smelling. There was one candle burning under a crucifix, and there at a table, her head cushioned on her arms, was Jean Hedley. The priest closed the door, and they were alone.

He went to her and put his hand on her glossy black hair. She looked up, and her eyes were dry. She said, "Thank you for coming, Ross."

There was little he could say. He fumbled nervously with his hat, and said, "I thought maybe there might be relatives back home—we could ship the body. Would you like that, Jean?"

She reached out and took his right hand in both of hers, and squeezed hard until the nails bit into his flesh. She said, "As long as I can remember, Mother talked of the day when Dad would finally settle down, and we would have a place of our own and live like other people. It was the one thing she wanted; it was the one thing that kept her going. She thought we had it when Bret came home and said we could buy the Tozier place. And then everything happened so fast, so crazy——" She stopped, and her voice broke slightly. She said, "Ross, I want to believe that Mother knew nothing at all about Bret. She had a way of shutting out things she didn't want to see, and I want to think that she shut that out too. I want to think she died believing we finally did have a place we could call our own, and that everything was going to be all right. I'd like to bury her on that knoll in back of the Tozier house where the valley sweeps down toward the river."

"We can do that, Jean," he said softly.

She got up then, and came toward him, and he put out his arms and held her close. She started to cry. Not heart-broken sobs. She cried softly, like a girl who is very tired. She leaned forward, and he bent his head, his lips touch-ing her hair. She said, "I don't want to go back to Dad, Ross. I can't—not right now."

"You come over to Judge Iverson's with me," he said. "Maria's there; she'll be good for you."

He left his horse at the church, and walked with her down the tree-lined street. They said nothing; somehow his hand found hers, and they walked that way, hand in hand. Feeling the press of Jean's hand against his, he wondered at the emotion that was everywhere in him.

17

HE WENT to the undertaker first, and made arrangements for Maw Hedley's funeral. In accordance with Jean's wishes, he explained, there would be no one at the burial except Sam and Jean. She seemed completely torn be-tween loyalty to her father and what she felt was his guilt for what had happened. It was a problem she wanted to work out alone, and Ross had offered no suggestions.

He avoided Ben Fransen's, for going there would only lead to trouble. So instead he went to Jim East's, the first time since the night he had killed Vance Levitt.

There were no more than a dozen men in the saloon; they were men Ross had never seen before, broad-hand-ed, wind-burned men, with the unmistakable mark of the plow about them. He exchanged brief greetings with East, then, sidling near a couple of men who might have been father and son, he offered to buy them a drink.

They accepted with an embarrassed geniality and the older man said, "Here's to you, feller."

Ross tipped his glass. "Farmers, are you?"

"Wheat," the younger man said. "Any objections?"

Ross shrugged. "Not me. I'm fence-building."

"For Warrington?" the old man wanted to know.

"That's right," Ross said. "Know him?"

"Know him?" the old man said. "Hell, yes!" He motioned to the bartender to fill Ross's glass. "One of the smartest wheat men I ever met in my life. Common as an old shoe once you get to know him. Hell, he was right at my supper table last night. Close as from me to you. Had a big meetin' over there to my place." The man stopped and pressed a stubby forefinger against Ross's chest. "Say," he speculated. "You ain't startin' the Catclaw fence already, are you?"

Ross shook his head, "North line."

The old man said, "Oh," apparently disappointed.

He had two more drinks with them, and met a half-dozen more of the wheat ranchers. They were all big, slow-moving, amiable men with a strange mixture of determination and dreams in their eyes. He liked them instinctively.

In time he got around to what was on his mind—the hiring of a crew; they turned him down, one by one. One answer was much like the next: "Warrington is helpin' us get some gang plows and disk harrows in here. We'll be breakin' ground in a month and up to that time we'll be right busy."

The young farmer was more frank than the others. "What we're after is that Catclaw fence, and Warrington says he'll put it in. He's already fenced in his south line and that's all we need. We don't know much about cows and brands, mister, except that one cow eats as much wheat as another. Don't reckon we'd be interested in gettin' mixed up in no fight between cow outfits."

It was useless trying to hire them, and after a couple of drinks more, Ross shook hands all around and left. He called on a couple of old-timers he knew in town, but they turned him down flat. "I'm gettin' too old for gunsmoke, Ross," said one. So by late evening he headed for Hogtown as the last resort.

He still had the money in his shirt, with the exception of the thousand dollars he had left with Lenore, and he was uneasy as he crossed the slough and went up the dimly lit street. He passed the deadfalls and bagnios without incident and came to the last block. He crossed the small ditch and saw what he imagined was the house of Gomez. It was dark.

He rapped on the door. From inside an old voice said, "*Quién es?*"

"Ross Parnell. Maria sent me."

The door opened carefully, a small crack, and the voice said, "What you want, Señor?"

"If you're Gomez, I want to talk to you. I'm a good friend of Maria's."

There was a long hesitation, a guarded movement inside, and then the door opened and let him in. The old Mexican fussed with a candle, and finally got it going; it threw a weird half-light around the single-room shack that held a stove, a bed, a chair and table, and a cupboard made of a packing box.

He was a gnarled gnome of a man, this Gomez, with a thin hatchet face and a scraggly white mustache. His black eyes, jewel-bright, kept darting furtively around. "Maria is my cousin," he explained senselessly.

"Yeah, I know," Ross said. "She tells me you are the best fence builder in the country."

Gomez thought that over for some time, then he pursed his withered lips, smacked them, nodded his birdlike head, and admitted frankly, "Is true."

"I'm starting to put that north fence through," Ross said. "She thought maybe I could get you to work for me."

Gomez shook his head vigorously. "I think I gonna go away someplace."

"She said you'd make a good straw boss. Help me round up a crew—be in charge of the men."

Gomez's eyes widened. "Straw boss?"

"That's right. *Patron.*"

Gomez laced his hands behind his back and walked up and down the room. "Straw boss," he said.

"You know any good men we could get?" Ross asked, building himself a cigarette. "I'd have to leave that up to you, of course." He walked over and started to sit down on the bed. Gomez grabbed his arm quickly and steered him to the single rawhide-bottomed chair. He seemed highly nervous. Ross, looking across the room now, saw a foot sticking out from under the bed. He grinned in spite of himself, and remembering how things had always been with the law in the Mexican section of Hogtown he said, "There's only one thing, Gomez. I'd want you to know about it before you went to work for me. I had a little argument with Sheriff Yates. Him and me don't get along very well. Now, if the sheriff is a friend of yours——"

"*Ay, caramba,* that shereef!" Gomez squealed. "He's loco in the head, that fella." The old Mexican went to the window, peered out into the darkness (though it would have been completely impossible to see anything), came back, and, leaning close to Ross, put his hand alongside his mouth and said, "The shereef is not my friend."

"Loco," Ross agreed, tapping his temple with a forefinger.

"Straw boss, eh? said Gomez.

"Hire anybody you want."

"Tell 'em what to do?"

"Tell 'em what to do."

Gomez inhaled deeply, pulling strength for the decision into his lungs. He hit himself on the chest with his clenched fist and said, "I take the job!"

Ross said, "How about the one under the bed—he want a job?"

Gomez was not the least bit disturbed. He kicked at the protruding foot and called, "Chico! Morales! come out from under the bed."

There was a delayed scrambling, a complaint of springs, the soft thud of a head against board. Two Mexicans came out from under the bed and looked at Ross sheepishly. Gomez shrugged his shoulders. "Crazy thing," he said. "Rather sleep on the floor than the bed." The old man pointed a palm-up hand to first one and then the other. He introduced them: "Chico—Morales. Two very best fence builders." The two men stood up, grinned, and said nothing.

Ross got to his feet. "I'm Ross Parnell," he said. He shook hands with each of the three in turn. "You know where the fence camp is, Gomez. If you can line up some more men, we can use 'em."

"*Si*, we can use 'em," Gomez said, nodding vigorously. "I gotta get me a pretty good-size crew." He was thoughtful a minute, then spoke rapidly in Spanish to Chico and Morales, and once or twice Ross thought he heard Sheriff Yates mentioned. When Gomez was through, the two men shrugged their shoulders. Gomez said to Ross, "I have my crew at camp tomorrow night."

Ross said good night gravely, and left, not completely satisfied with what he had accomplished, but certainly a lot further ahead than he had been. For all he knew Chico and Morales might be guilty of murder, but it was a lot more probable that the sheriff had a chicken-stealing warrant in his pocket for them. At the moment Ross didn't particularly give a damn—he needed men.

He recrossed the little ditch and started up the dim street back toward the center of Hogtown. He had gone less than half a block when he had the uncomfortable feeling of being followed. He reached inside his shirt and pushed the packet of money down to where his belt would bind it, then, pulling his hat low, he quickened his footsteps. A short, stocky man came out from behind a building and stood in the street in front of him. Ross moved onto the sidewalk, alert to every sound. The man in the street matched his move. There was a dark, foul-smelling space between two buildings, and as he came to that, Ross thought he saw a movement there in the darkness. He half-turned, ready to dodge, and saw that the short, stocky man was diving in toward him. At the same time a second man lunged out of the shadows of the alley.

Ross whirled in his steps, thinking to get out in the open, into more light. A fist slashed out and caught him a vicious blow on the side of the head, knocking him to his knees. The short, stocky man closed in, swinging.

Stunned by the first blow, Ross fought by instinct only. He felt his fist land solidly once, and the jar of it seemed to snap him back to his senses. The tall, gangling man who had been in the alley came charging in, and Ross met him with a hard, short blow that cracked against a muscle-tight middle. The tall man connected a fist against Ross's mouth, but there was little strength in the blow.

The shorter man of the two was having trouble getting to his feet. Ross kicked out, catching that one on the jaw with his boot heel, and then he turned his attention to the tall man. The tall one swung a long, looping right that missed, and Ross countered with a quick left hook that cracked against bone. The man went down, and didn't move.

Ross rolled, expecting to meet the onslaught of the second thug, but that one was making no move to continue the fight. He said, "The hell with it. You're more than a ten-buck job."

Ross grasped the man by the shirt front, jerking him forward, holding him close. He cocked his right fist and said, "All right, start talking."

The short man said, "No savvy English."

There was something about his attitude that kept Ross from hitting him. He seemed to be treating the whole affair as a legitimate business proposition that had back-fired. The tall one groaned and sat up. He said, "A hell of a way to earn ten bucks."

Ross had a chance to size them up then. Cowpunchers, undoubtedly, way down on their luck. Their clothes were brush-torn and saddle-dirty, and as he got a better look at them he got the feeling that neither one of them had had a square meal for a long time. One was tall, stringy, bowlegged, and hawk-faced. The other was solid-ly built, a dark man with a face that might have been called mean. But at the moment he had a comical, re-signed-to-fate expression that made him appear almost humorous. Ross said, "Ben Fransen hire you to waylay me?"

The tall one said, "I ain't good at names."

The picture was simple. Fransen, still playing it smart, had hired a couple of down-and-out saddle bums, giving them a chance to earn a meal and a few drinks. He had probably told them he wanted somebody roughed up and let it go at that. The drifters would be out of town by morning and Ross would have nothing worse than a sore jaw and a busted head, which, in Hogtown, wouldn't be anything to stir excitement. It would be mighty hard for anyone to prove what happened to the money he carried. Instinct made him reach to see if the packet was still there; then, following his hunch, he hauled the money out of his shirt front and held it where the two men could see. He said, "You after this?"

The tall man looked at the money and his voice had a steely bite to it. He said, "Hold tight a minute, friend. We don't roll our customers."

"Looks to me like somebody played you for a couple of suckers," Ross said. "Everybody in town knows I'm packing this money; if it turned up missing, I reckon the sheriff would be looking for a couple of drifters that passed through here in a hurry."

The short one said, "I smell skunk."

Ross ran his thumb across the edge of the bills. He said, "Like some of this?"

"Go to hell," said the tall one. "Tromp your own snakes."

Ross said, "No head bustin', and good chow. Fence-building."

"Where I come from," said the short one, "they say fence and fight all in the same breath."

"Could be they do here too," replied Ross. "You don't look like that would scare you. I'll start you off with a couple of drinks and a good steak."

"I like steak," said the tall one.

They shook hands then, and the three of them went down the street together. The only comment made was when the short one scratched his head and said, "Damned if this ain't the craziest place we hit yet."

Ross took them down to Jim East's; as they came into the light in front of the saloon, he handed the tall one a ten-dollar bill and said, "Call this an advance on your first month's wages."

Both men looked at him quickly and for the first time they grinned. The tall one said, "They call me Stuffy. This here's Galt."

Ross gave them his name, then, pointing out the Swensen Construction Company warehouse down by the river, he said, "I got some supplies to pick up. Meet me down by that little office shack in about an hour." He turned and left them; somehow he felt they'd be there.

And in just less than an hour Stuffy and Galt, faces washed and stomachs full, were loading rolls of barbed wire on three stake-bed wagons down in the Swensen yard. Inside the office the old watchman looked over the top of his desk into the barrel of Ross Parnell's .44. His eyes said he had a healthy respect for the finger that was around the trigger, but his voice didn't quaver. He said, "I told you you'd have to talk to Fransen about buying this stuff."

"Look, old-timer," Ross said softly. "I got nothing against you, and I didn't want to get rough. But Fransen has decided what rules to play by, and it's all right by me. My boys have cut out twelve head of mules and three of your wagons and we're loading with wire and staples." With his left hand Ross reached inside his shirt and pulled out the package of bills, somewhat diminished now from his purchase of grub, axes, shovels, and picks. He said, "If you want it that way, I'll stand here until we're loaded; I'd rather be out there helping. Show me what Fransen paid for this stuff, and I'll leave money enough to cover everything I'm taking. Behave yourself and there'll be an extra twenty-dollar bill."

The old man thought it over for a while, shrugged, and said, "Well, if that's the way you do business, bub."

And shortly after midnight three wagons, loaded with wire and staples and a good supply of groceries, pulled out of Saboba and crossed the Sasinaw. By dawn they were near the end of the north fence line, and Ross and Stuffy and Galt were talking of sleep.

18

It STARTED raining around the first of the week, and by Friday night the ground had taken all it would hold; still the skies continued to drench the prairie. Ross worked a heavy chain around a bundle of posts; his hand slipped, and skin ripped off his knuckles for the twentieth time that day. He tested the chain's grip, grunted in satisfaction, and straightened up. Devils of fatigue pain danced across his back and drove molten lead into his legs. The water streamed off his mud-caked yellow slicker, and when he tilted his head to see the top of the cliff, the rain beat into his eyes and ran in trickles down the gray, tired furrows of his face.

He had done a lot in less than a week. Galt and Stuffy and the six Mexicans old Gomez had brought with him had turned out to be as fine a crew as a man could ask for, but at best he had no more than a third of the men he needed for the job. He had put Stuffy and Galt to work felling cottonwoods. They had grumbled and complained, and the first day raised blisters the size of silver dollars on their hands. But they stuck to it, and were starting to get the swing of things.

Page and Farrel, the two XR men, had stayed three days doing nothing; Ross had sent them back to Sellew with a note of thanks to Lenore and an invitation to her to come out and see how things were going.

Now he was beginning to worry: a few more days of this rain and the canyon he had picked as a post-cutting site would be a roaring creek bed, and the small amount of work he had accomplished would be gone. He jerked the chain three times, and the bound bundle of posts started to slip up the mud-running wall of the canyon.

All week it had been like this, fourteen hours a day. He had to keep at it if he wanted to keep his small cutting of posts from washing down the canyon, to pile up like a jumble of matches on a bunkhouse poker table. And even more relentless than the rain was the ominous lack of activity from the direction of Saboba. He had fully expected Fransen to send Sheriff Yates out with a warrant for his arrest, and he had just as fully decided to tear the warrant up in the sheriff's face. But as yet, nothing had happened, and it was more of a strain than if Fransen had come out with blazing guns. He couldn't decide whether Fransen was ashamed to admit his loss or was so supremely confident of himself that he didn't care. It was probably the latter, Ross thought bitterly.

Up on the lip of the canyon, Gomez, the old Mexican, lashed at his team of mules, and their hoofs bit into the slime of the mud, and the chain became taut. The mules leaned into the collar, and, down at the bottom of the wall, the bundle of posts started up. The Mexican grinned, letting the rain drip off the end of his mustache.

As soon as the posts were up on top they would be loaded onto one of the wagons by the waiting crew of two, to be hauled out and distributed along the proposed fence line. While the men loaded the wagon the chain would go back down to where Ross and his four helpers would have another bundle of posts ready; everything had to move with precision.

In the drenching breaks at the bottom of the canyon Ross and his four men packed newly cut posts from the brush, and laid them on a crude cradle at the base of the cliff. With this loading table he had figured out he could make up the load and have it ready by the time the chain came down. Then all they had to do was slip the chain around the bundle, secure it, and signal old Gomez to start the team.

The four men came out of the thicket, each man packing a post on his shoulder, walking at almost a dogtrot. In their yellow slickers they all looked alike, but under the beard and mud Ross knew that two of them were Anglos and two of them were Mexicans and he wondered what difference it made. He had made up a sort of pay roll and on that roll their names were down simply as Chico, Morales, Stuffy, and Galt. It hadn't looked quite formal enough, so Ross had put a mister in front of each name and let it go at that. None of the four looked as if he wanted to be pressed for formality, but he'd go a long way to find better workers, and at the moment that was all that counted.

He looked up into the rain, cursed a little as he saw the bundle of posts jerk crazily. "That damn Gomez must think them mules are race horses," he grumbled good-naturedly.

The rain made a thunderous racket in his ears. The two Mexicans and Stuffy and Galt tossed their posts into the pile. The posts thudded noisily, the pile shifted, and other posts rolled against the cradle. The rain pounded so hard now they had to shout to one another, but Ross caught the high-pitched yell from the top of the cliff. He cocked his head, trying to hear more. A crazy fear grabbed at the pit of his stomach. The post-cutters had gone back into the thicket for another load. "Nerves," Ross said sullenly. "The minute I get these damn posts out of the canyon I'm gonna sleep for a week."

Actually, he knew there'd be no rest until the fence was built and the XR had paid him off. When that fence was in, Lenore Warrington and the small ranchers would have no reason to fight. He felt both sides wanted peace; if Ben Fransen still wanted trouble, then it would show him up for exactly what Ross suspected him to be: a big-scale rustler who saw in barbed wire his worst enemy. Ross was perfectly willing to make it personal between Fransen and himself then, but not as long as it might mean setting off the short fuse that led to the war of misunderstanding hovering over the valley.

Now he waited impatiently in the bottom of the canyon, wondering what was holding Gomez. It took only a few minutes to unfasten the chain, get the mules back to the edge of the cliff, and drop the chain down for another load. The men, dulled into pieces of machinery by fatigue, had gotten to the point where they did things automatically, without a hitch.

The sky had turned pitch black, and the rain had doubled in intensity so that when he looked up he couldn't see what was going on up there on the rim of the canyon. He knew only that Gomez was taking too much time. And then again, after a while, he felt that fear lace through his belly.

Galt and the others came out of the thicket. They stood there, hollow-eyed, saying nothing, rain streaming from their faces. Ross could see the questions in their minds when they noticed the chain had not been dropped. "Have to go up there and wake 'em up, I guess," Ross said by way of conversation.

The Mexican Ross called Chico grinned widely and said, "My leetle brother José, he's a lazy one. I tole you he should be down here where I can keek heem in the pants."

Conversation—just something to say. But at the end of ten minutes there was no more conversation between the four men there at the bottom of the canyon. Something was wrong up on top, and they knew it. "Someone hurt, maybe," Galt said.

Improbable as hell, Ross knew. The posts, heavy as they were, weren't likely to cause anyone any serious damage. The possibility of a load shifting on one of the stake-bed wagons was mighty remote. If trouble had hit the post camp it was trouble that was not accidental, and every man there knew it.

The long, lanky cowpuncher called Stuffy said, "You want I should go up and have a look-see, boss?"

Ross tried to sound offhand about it. He said, "Getting pretty late anyway. We all better go up. We'll load up the kid so he can get an early start in the morning. That way we won't waste no time."

"Sure, that's all right," Galt said. Ross noticed Galt had pushed his slicker aside and adjusted the gun belt he always wore, even when working. The others went over to the small tarp-covered lean-to they had built. Chico came back with a shotgun that seemed to be a constant part of him, "because I might see a duck," as he put it.

The one called Morales never appeared to carry a weapon, but Ross had the feeling that a close examination would disclose a knife in his boot and another inside his shirt. Stuffy and Galt were both six-shooter men and made no bones about it. Ross never packed a gun on the job.

Together, then, the five of them climbed the zigzagging trail they had cut in the side of the canyon wall. Ross took the lead, Chico, with his double-barreled shotgun, bringing up the rear. The wind shifted around and the rain beat straight into their faces, sliming the mud underfoot, sending it in increasing red rivers down the face of the cliff.

They had no business knocking off this early, Ross knew, but by now there was no doubt that something was wrong. They slipped and slid, and pulled themselves up the last steep jog of the trail to the top of the canyon. There the soggy, spongy mesa stretched out, table-flat, sloping finally down toward the Sasinaw and the broad valley.

The mules were standing there, still hitched to their load of posts; the Mexican crew was not in sight. Ross started toward the sagging tent they had fixed for a cook shack; old Gomez met him at the door, a rifle in his hand. The old man said, "I was just coming down to get you, Señor Ross. Something happening out there." He jerked his head toward the breaks to the east.

"What is it?"

"Come away from the tent where the rain don't pound so hard. You can hear."

Ross went inside the tent first, got his gun belt and strapped it on. The other Mexicans were inside the tent, waiting for orders. He took Stuffy and Galt with him, and with Gomez they walked across the spongy mesa to where the rain was only a whisper against the grass.

Gomez stopped suddenly, put his hand on Ross's arm. "Listen!"

They strained their ears for a second, and the men exchanged glances. It was unmistakable—the bawling of cattle: a good-sized herd on the move.

"When I work on the fence before, I hear this," Gomez said. "I hear this the night Ed Tozier get killed."

Ross nodded quickly. Darkness was settling fast. "Get your horses," he said. "We'll take a look-see."

Figuring it might possibly be a trap to get him out of camp, he left Stuffy in charge of the Mexican crew, and took Gomez, Galt, and Chico with him. The four men rode down the steep wall of the mesa into the thick, drenched country that lay at the bottom of the next canyon. Here they could detect the bawl of the cattle even above the beat of the rain. They stopped to get the direction; Gomez made a motion with his hand, indicating one canyon over and more to the east. From that point cross-canyons could easily lead either across Diego Palomar's or Ed Tozier's place, then north to the railroad.

There was a thick, soupy darkness settling over the canyons now, making going difficult. Ross calculated the time it would take to get over the next ridge, then decided to head due east, down the canyon they were in, hoping thereby to intercept the herd.

They worked by sound and guesswork, and in time they picked up the shouts of men and the bellowing of the cattle—loud enough that they knew they hadn't been wrong. They waited a half-hour that seemed an eternity, and then, ahead of the cattle, they heard the single horse. Ross gave the word, and heard rifles clear saddle scabbards. He stood in his stirrups and called into the rain.

There was no human reply: nothing but the bawl of the cattle and the complaint of the weather. Then, suddenly, close by, a gun cracked, and lead whined by his head.

Both Galt and Chico fired at the muzzle blast. For a dead second the cattle were completely silent; Ross could picture them, standing stiff-legged and wide-eyed, Somewhere, a distance off, men shouted to one another. Then there was a sudden shifting of weight, a pounding of hoofs. Ross heard another rifle shot, then the full, surging impact of the cattle terrorized into a frenzied stampede.

Ross pulled his men deeper into the canyon, more anxious now to keep away from that earth-jarring rush of maddened beasts than he was to discover the identity of the rustlers.

The air was full of the thudding, sucking sound of hoofs, the clacking of horns, the stench of overheated animals. The stampede was visible only as a black, undulating mass rushing crazily north like a flood-swollen river, not knowing nor caring where it ran.

A rider, then, distinguishable only by the fact that it was a different shape in the lumpy darkness. Ross fired a warning shot. Three rifles answered the challenge. Then a quick, flashing exchange—inky blackness, moving targets—there was no aiming, no strategy. If a man was hit it would be because there was lead in the air and he was at the wrong place at the wrong time.

But a man was hit. Ross knew it by the scream of pain, then knew it for sure when the riderless horse turned into the canyon and ran close enough so that Chico was able to run out and grasp the trailing reins.

The cattle were still running, maddened, and the riders were following now, trying to get to an open place where they could head them. Ross and his men waited, crouched in the brush, and in a half-hour there was nothing but the thunder of the rain and the fast-diminishing mumble of a fear-crazed herd.

They came out of cover then, cautiously, ears alert to every sound, eyes strained for movement. "One was hit," Ross said. "I want to find him." Gomez nodded. They split and started working their way on foot across the floor of the canyon. Ross felt his heart beating steadily, high in his chest. The rain became an unbearable sound that was worse than silence.

Suddenly the ugly crack of a gun, a spit of flame, the quick sound of a struggle; then Chico's voice, high-pitched, elated. "Come queek! I got heem!"

Ross broke into a run and heard the others closing in. He found Chico astride a man, face down in the mud. Chico said, "He try to shoot me, but I get heem. He's plenty shot."

A sickness started in the pit of Ross Parnell's stomach. He fought against it, tried to keep the trembling out of his hands. He dropped down on his knees in the mud and rolled the dying man over on his back. He knew now, without looking—it was Bret Hedley.

19

IT WAS DIM morning when Ross Parnell rode his XR horse into an XR-hating town. He knew everything he needed to know now, and there was a hard, driving hatred in him that wiped every bit of expression from his face and left nothing but a gray, drawn mask that held a bitter, almost brutal intensity.

Bret Hedley had talked before he died; he had cried like a baby. Over and over in the last seconds of life that were left to him he tried to offer some explanation as to why he had killed Ed Tozier. It was as if, in that fraction of time that was left, the kid was trying to piece together every move that had gone wrong in his life.

Watching him there in the mud, clutching at the jagged hole in his chest, fighting for words, Ross had seen a lot of Jean in the kid's eyes, a lot of Sam in the set of his face.

Ross said finally, "Don't talk any more, Bret. It's all right." The kid's last word had been Jean's name.

So he knew, now. Knew that it was Ben Fransen in back of the large-scale raids, knew that it was Trip Levitt who was doing the actual work. At first it had been from inside the XR, and then, after Levitt was fired, they had gone on operating with the help of a single spy in the XR bunkhouse. And he knew, too, that Tony Sellew had nothing to do with it; that Tony was playing a separate game, hoping to break up the Warringtons, then move in and marry Lenore. His ambition was as determined as was Ben Fransen's, but he was playing it alone. Ross knew a lot of things now. He could prove nothing, but there are other things a man can do.

The rain had let up some; he crossed the bridge, past the warehouse and the yard where the wire was stored. He rode up the main street, turned left, and came to Judge Iverson's house, set behind its picket fence. He dismounted and went to the door. Maria let him in. He said only, "I want to see the girl."

Maria called her; she came to the door of the bedroom, a blanket over her shoulders, drawn around her night clothes. All the way in he had tried to figure some way to tell her, some way to take the hurt out of it. But now, as he saw her, he knew that anything less than the truth would not be enough. All that frank, uninhibited honesty was in her face now. There was both hope and fear in her eyes.

There was no surge of emotion in him. There was no feeling whatsoever. He went to her and put his arms around her and he tilted her chin and kissed her on the lips. And then he told her, speaking slowly, leaving nothing unsaid. When he was finished she looked at him, her eyes dry, her face dead white. Her voice was a whisper. She said, "Thank you, Ross." She went back in the bedroom and closed the door behind her.

And at that second the driving, surging, devil urge to kill was as strong in Ross Parnell as he had ever felt it.

He turned to leave, and heard Judge Iverson calling to him. He was short with the judge, saying only what was necessary. The judge said, "You've got the word of a dead man, Ross: it might not mean much in court."

"There'll be no court," Ross said.

The judge said, "Fransen has got Palomar and Murdock and Baudry stringing with him now. Don't start something you can't stop."

"I'll see you later, Judge," Ross said, and he went outside.

He rode back to the main street and turned to the right. Saboba was still asleep. He tied his horse in front of Jim East's saloon, three doors from the corner. He went inside, had three whiskies, and paid for them. It was too early for the bartender to be talkative. After that Ross went back outside, walked around the corner, and stopped in front of the third building. The dripping cloth sign that half-covered the front of the building said BEN FRANSEN—LAND LOCATOR AND LICENSED SURVEYOR. Then, under that in smaller letters, Real Estate Loans. Ross stepped back, then lunged against the flimsy panel of the door. Twice more, and a hasp splintered from the jam; the door flew open, spilling him halfway across the room.

The office was cluttered; a flat table near the far corner was covered with a mass of papers; there was a tin can half full of cigar stubs—the reek of them hung over the entire office; behind the table was a chair, with one leg broken—it had been wired together; a heavy bow-back chair stood near the door—the kind common to barrooms —and in the opposite corner was a substantial hall tree, finished in golden oak. An earthen *olla* of water rested on a small stand.

Ross shot his hand out and swept the papers and the

can of cigar stubs from the top of the table. After that he stood there, breathing heavily, then picked up the hall tree and smashed it against the earthen water jug; the jug splintered into a dozen pieces and the water trickled out onto the floor. He picked up the barroom chair and started beating it against the top of the table; the top split—the table collapsed. It was no trick to wrench off one of the legs. With that he broke everything in the place; in a small closet he found the surveying instruments, which he smashed beyond recognition.

His lips were drawn tight against his teeth now. Sweat born of rage and hopeless fatigue streamed from his body, soaked his shirt, and trickled down the back of his legs. He took the hall tree again and punched out the two front windows with it, then managed to wrench the door off its hinges. Dust blew up from the floor and stung his nostrils.

When he stepped outside into the air, he found a ring of white-faced men standing there, watching him. They backed away a few steps as he came out on the sidewalk. He told them, "My fight is with Ben Fransen—nobody else. You boys keep out of it." His order included Murdock and Palomar, a couple of their men, and some XR punchers who were still in town. He noticed several wheat men, back to one side.

He went straight to Fransen's saloon and had two more drinks. The bartender kept watching him, licking his lips. A man he didn't know came in off the street, glanced furtively at Ross, then ran upstairs. And in a short while he heard the slow, measured footsteps coming down.

Fransen appeared at the foot of the stairs, walked across the barroom, stood there, saying nothing. Unshaven, his face had a blue-black look that had lost its color. His thickset nose seemed to hunch out from between his eyes and the thick brows made a solid line across his forehead. His mouth was full and loose and moist, shaped around that eternal heavy cigar. He came up to the bar and stood beside Ross. Gib Baudry came in off the street and stood there by the bar. The bartender shoved Fransen a glass, but he waved it aside. "I hear you want trouble, Parnell," he said. Gib Baudry moved a step closer.

Ross said, "I'm building a fence, Fransen. I contracted to build it. I don't take orders from the XR nor any other man. When that fence is built, it will cut into your cow stealin' and tame things down in the valley. Then there won't be such a turnover in land, and it won't be so good for you. I had a long talk with Bret Hedley before he died. I don't like what you did to that kid; I'm here to tell you so."

There was a quick intake of breath from the crowd. Ben Fransen moved away from the bar, his fists clenched, his feet wide spread. He made a quick lunge; as he did he said, "Take him, Gib!" Ross pivoted, turning his back on Fransen. He sunk his fist wrist-deep into the belly of Gib Baudry, who was charging in from the other side.

Baudry made a thick, gurgling sound in his throat, and stepped back, blinking. He was a good three inches shorter than Ross and a good three inches wider. His shirt was unbuttoned halfway down the front, exposing his gray underwear; his sleeves were rolled to his elbows. He shifted his weight now, spreading his feet; his bullet-like head seemed to sink lower, telescoping his thick neck. His hand shot out, scooped a bottle from the bar, threw it. Ross ducked and came barging in.

For a second they were locked there, heads against shoulders. Then Baudry's knee came up sharply, catching Ross in the stomach. Ross lost his grip and staggered backward, tripped, and fell on his back; Fransen's big henchman came in for the kill.

Fransen was standing with both elbows on the bar now, cool and unconcerned, the cigar jutting upward out of the corner of his mouth. There was an amused look on his face. He had perfect confidence in the prowess of Gib Baudry. The other men had crowded into the saloon, and stood there in a circle. Regardless of what their feelings in the matter might be, this was Ross Parnell's fight; they wouldn't step into it.

Baudry gripped the bar with his right hand, supporting himself; he raised his boot to tromp it against Parnell's face. Ross saw it coming, rolled, grabbed at the boot and pulled it loose. Quick as a cat, he was on his feet. He threw the boot, and it smashed against the side of Gib Baudry's head, leaving a bright red patch of ripped skin.

Baudry's right hand left the bar, swung in a wide arc, and caught Ross on the side of the face. Ross went stumbling backward and fell against a table; he could see Baudry coming after him. Gripping the edge of the table with both hands, he drew his knees up against his chest and kicked out with both feet; the blow caught Baudry in the chest, sprawling him back against the bar. Ross dropped to his feet, picked up a chair and swung it with all his weight. Baudry turned, and the chair splintered against his massive shoulders. They stood there then, toe to toe, slugging; each blow ripped skin, and thudded with the sickening grind of ruined flesh.

But Ross was feeling no pain. He could take a beating like this for the next two hours, he knew, and he wouldn't go down under it. It had been coming for a week, building up, driving him crazy with worry and fatigue. Now it had happened, and men had died; this fighting was like a tonic singing in his veins, driving him on.

Baudry missed a long, looping swing, and for a second his chin was exposed; Ross didn't miss the opportunity. He saw Baudry's head snap back, saw his mouth drop open. He followed through quickly, his knuckles ripping against the exposed teeth. Baudry's tongue came out, and the blood ran down both sides of his chin.

Ross let him have it again, but Baudry was still a long way from gone; he started backing toward the door now, a bullish ape of a man refusing to go down, and refusing to quit. His blows were jerkier, more measured, but they had just as much power behind them, and keeping away from their danger made Ross's slugging ineffective.

Baudry got his hands on a chair and swung it down in time for Ross's fist to smash against the heavy bottom. Hot shivers of pain hammered against Parnell's elbow and screamed up into his shoulder, but he gripped the rungs of the chair with both hands, leaning his weight against it. They stood there that way rocking back and forth. Then Ross released his grip suddenly, and Baudry stumbled forward. Ross sidestepped, and smashed the edge of his hand wickedly against the broad back of that thick boil-pitted neck. He heard Baudry's guttural cough of pain, and, stepping back again, Ross lifted the man's head with a hard smash in the face.

After that Baudry started giving way. He backed on through the door, across the hard-packed sidewalk and into the muddy street. He stood there, swinging wildly, hitting nothing; Ross followed, smashing him again and again until Baudry went down on his knees, then over backward into the mud.

Still Ross followed him, and they rolled there until those on the sidewalk could not tell which man was which; until, finally, one stood up and walked away without ever looking back. They knew that this was Ross Parnell.

For the first time Ben Fransen took the cigar from his mouth. He ground it out under his foot, then walked over to where Gib Baudry lay face down in the mud. Fransen's voice was thick with disgust. He nudged Baudry over with his foot and said, "Get up, damn you, before I kick your face in." Then he turned and went back toward the saloon.

On the sidewalk men split into two groups, and spoke in low tones. A bunch of XR punchers swaggered onto the street as if defying anyone to get in their way. Murdock and Palomar stared at the retreating back of Ross Parnell.

20

ROSS WAS SICK: he felt like the insides had been shaken out of him, and he remembered that once he had ridden an outlaw bronc, and afterward had felt something like this. He knew they were watching him there in front of Fransen's saloon, and he couldn't let himself down yet, so he walked straight around the corner back to where he had left his horse. He got into the saddle and rode up to Court Street, then left two blocks; when the cottonwood at that corner hid him he dismounted and let himself go.

After that he was weak and trembling and he knew that his face was colorless except for the raw, red bruises. He kept thinking of Bret and of Jean, and he realized suddenly that lately whenever trouble was thickest he thought of Jean. He didn't bother to wipe the blood from his hands and face nor did he try to rebutton the torn shirt that failed to cover the red welts on his body. He didn't have to pretend with Jean, nor with the judge.

He rode to the white picket fence that stood half as high as the hollyhocks and went inside the yard, leaving the gate open behind him. The porch boards complained beneath his weight, and the front door opened before he had a chance to knock. It was Jean, and she said, "Come in, Ross. I've got some water heating on the stove. Take off your shirt and come in the kitchen." He didn't argue.

She wore a blue-and-white-checked gingham dress that had a bit of fluff around the high neckline and on the short puffed sleeves. It was a plain and practical dress, with a single row of buttons that ran from the high collar to the tight waist. The skirt came to her shoetops. There were a thousand dresses like it in the country, but he remembered thinking there must be only one girl who could wear one the way she wore it. He was strangely at peace, even in the middle of turmoil.

She bathed his face without speaking to him and she took a comb and ran it through his hair, pulling it back out of his eyes. After that she poured him a glass of whisky. It wasn't until then that she spoke. She said, "What now, Ross?"

They heard the creak of a door, the slow, shuffling footsteps. The judge, supported by Maria, fully dressed, his long, black coat draped over his shoulders, came into the room. His face was drawn with pain, but there was something about the set of his expression that reminded Ross of the old fire that had made this man so long a leader in Saboba. He looked at Ross and said, "You'll need help now, boy. There's five men on my place, and they're yours. Those three boys who worked for Ed Tozier are in town; they'll string along. I'll try to make Dan Murdock and Don Diego see it the same way. Fransen won't give up easy—he's got too much to lose."

"He'll need more help than he's got to make much of a stand," Ross said.

The judge said, "Get rid of that XR horse you're riding. Murdock is pig-headed. It's Tony Sellew he's afraid of, and Fransen's been playing that for all it's worth. Selley was in town one day this week, drunk. He told everybody who would listen that Warrington had pulled out, and he figured it wouldn't be long before Lenore would be Mrs. Tony Sellew. He made it plain that when that happened there'd be some boundary changes on the XR.

Maybe it was whisky talking, but it scared a lot of people. The way things are they're more apt to make a hero out of a man who stole XR beef than they are to turn against him."

"I'll handle Sellew," said Ross.

He left them, and went back downtown; he made no attempt to get rid of the XR horse as the judge had advised. Rather than stirring Murdock and Palomar to more hatred of their big neighbor he felt it might make them reason and see things as he saw them. Actually, the small ranchers and the XR were after the same thing—a fence. And today he had tried to make it plain that it was Fransen alone who was fighting that fence. Fransen, who, his real estate business lagging, saw too late that a fence would put an end to his whipping the breaks for free beef. Fransen lived to make money, and when his means of money-making was threatened he was ready to fight. Today he wanted the legitimate ranchers of the valley to fight with him, and, out of the chaos of war he would find a way to make a profit. He always had. If siding with the XR would have made him a profit he would have been just as stanch an ally on that side. It was Judge Iverson's job to make Murdock and Palomar see that; somehow Ross felt the old man could do it.

He rode uninterrupted down the street. He saw that Warrington was in town with a dozen of his wheat-rancher friends. He wanted to talk to Warrington, but that would have to wait. He saw Sellew's horse in front of the saloon and was surprised to find the XR foreman was in town.

He was anxious to get back to his fence crew in case trouble should strike there, so he rode on. But when he had crossed the bridge and was a mile up the river, lack of sleep, the fatigue, and the beating he had taken all caught up with him and he was violently sick. He reined his horse into a thicket of willows, dismounted, and lay there in the soggy wet grass. He had no way of knowing how long he was there, but gradually the weak, trembling nausea went out of his stomach and he could stand on his feet without shaking.

He heard the sound of horses; the sharp instinct of danger that had been so much a part of him these last few days drove the last pain from his body. He led his horse farther into the thicket, and stood with his hand pinching the animal's nostrils.

The riders were close, coming down the trail that led to the XR. Water from the week's drench of rain slipped from the leaves and ran down the neck of his shirt. He moved cautiously, parting the bushes; his muscles were suddenly tight, his mouth dry.

He recognized a half-dozen XR punchers, but it was the two men riding in the lead that held him rigid. Riding side by side, one man looked like a coiled spring ready to burst into explosion. The other talked with his hands, spoke so softly that Ross could not hear what he said. He looked like a man who was selling a bushel of death for a high price. That coiled spring of a man was Tony Sellew, and the man who peddled death was Ben Fransen. As they passed him, he saw they were all heavily armed; they went on down the trail toward the XR. It would be crazy to try to find out anything now. He watched them gig their horses into a jogging trot, and waited until they were out of sight before he mounted and followed in the same direction.

An hour before sundown it started raining again—rolling, drenching squalls that rolled across the plains, dumping their tons of water, rumbling on southward. By the time Ross got back to the post camp he was soaked to the skin. He couldn't see any lights or any sign of a fire under the shed they had built—it worried him. Then a voice close by and soft said, "Hold up a minute, pardner. Let's take a look at you."

Ross let the air whoosh out of his lungs. He said, "It's me, Stuffy."

The long, lanky puncher materialized out of the darkness. He had a cocked six-shooter in his right hand. He let the hammer down easily and dropped the gun into its holster. Then he started talking, just as if there had never been an interruption in the conversation of the previous day. He said, "The letup in the rain give us a chance to get most of the posts on the bank. We worked on that all day. We didn't try to haul none out on the fence line."

"I appreciate it like hell, Stuffy," Ross said.

The puncher turned his back and said over his shoulder, "It's a job, ain't it?"

They weren't men you could go around praising and slapping on the back. A week ago Ross had knocked the head half off this man; since then there had been no mention of it. He had come to appreciate his crew, and had come to feel a real responsibility toward them. They were men who said nothing of their past and made no plans for the future, but they were men he could count on in a fight.

Chico, Morales, and Galt were rolled in their blankets under one of the wagons. They had dug a trench around themselves to try to keep off some of the water. Ross knew that all three of them were awake, watching him, but they didn't make a move. They knew how to save their energy until it was needed.

The next morning at a breakfast of cold biscuits and coffee they didn't ask for information; they waited until Ross told them. He tried to keep his voice light, making it sound as if their worries were over. But the nagging puzzle of Ben Fransen and Tony Sellew riding off toward the XR together had robbed him of another night's sleep. When men like Fransen and Sellew got together after hating each other so long, they got together for business reasons. And business with them meant trouble.

Finally Galt looked up from his coffee, a sympathetic grin on his face. He said, "You make it sound pretty as hell, boss. All that talk about how we'll raise hell in town for a week when the job's done and all. Why don't you believe it?"

Ross didn't have a chance to answer. Four riders had come up the XR side of the fence and dismounted about three hundred yards away. They looked as if they planned on making camp there. Ross waited until he was sure they weren't coming any farther, then strapped on his gun and went over to see what it was all about. Somehow, without being obvious, Galt fell in beside him. They looked as if they were merely checking the fence that had already been strung.

A short, hammered-down, bowlegged man came down the XR side of the fence to meet them. He was one of the men Ross had first seen with Trip Levitt. He recalled that this same man had ridden last night with Fransen and Sellew. When he was fifteen feet away from Ross the XR puncher stopped, leaned against one of the fence posts, and built himself a cigarette under the shield of his broad-brimmed hat. He was not looking at Ross, but was staring stolidly at Galt.

Galt said, "Hello, Rocky. Still hiring your gun out for cash money?"

The man called Rocky licked his cigarette, twisted the end of it, placed it carefully in his mouth, and said, "Yeah. How about you, Galt?"

"I got a job building fence," said Galt. "Any objection?"

"None, as long as you keep building fence. That jigger with you is Ross Parnell, ain't he?"

"That's him," Galt said.

"Me and my boys there work for Tony Sellew," the man called Rocky said, jerking his thumb toward the three who stood with hands on guns. "Sellew says you made some big talk about finishing this fence. We're here to see you do it. You need any supplies or grub, we'll bring it out to you. You stay the hell out of Saboba." He turned around deliberately and walked back to where the three gunhawks were waiting.

Ross started to take a step forward, but Galt laid a hand on his arm. "Leave him alone," Galt warned softly. "Him and them three with him are bad medicine. I knew 'em once over in New Mexico. Play it easy and see what they're up to."

The swift anger passed out of Ross quickly as he realized the sense in Galt's warning. The gunmen were on XR property and had every right to be there; this was no time to start a needless killing. He allowed himself a minute, waiting until the knot untied in the pit of his stomach, then said softly, "What the hell do you suppose that means?"

Galt shrugged. He said, "Maybe they just want to see your friend Fransen don't bother you no more."

"Maybe," Ross said.

They turned and went back to where Chico, Morales, and Stuffy were waiting. He still hadn't told them about seeing Fransen and Tony Sellew together. Some kind of a play was shaping up here that he couldn't quite catch. It kept gnawing at him, making him edgy, and when he saw a dozen riders loping in from the direction of Saboba he found his hand going to his six-shooter first, his thoughts coming later. When the riders were close enough, he recognized Dan Murdock and the riders from the small ranches.

Ross had a weak grin on his face when the men reined into the post camp. He said, "You should have sent word you was comin' out for a visit, Dan. I might have mistook you for buzzards and taken a shot at you."

Dan Murdock didn't smile. He said, "I'm man enough to admit it when I'm wrong, Ross. Palomar will send his boys over later. We'll try to round up a few more." He offered his hand.

Ross shook it warmly, and it brought a surge of well-being. He said, "How about Fransen and Baudry? Seen anything of them?"

"Baudry's around cryin' to come back into the fold. Looks like he was run through a meat grinder. Fransen has skipped town clean, so I reckon he's had enough. Looks like smooth sailin' all around now."

Ross glanced at the four XR men still over there by the fence line. He said, "You might as well know, Dan. I'm worried as hell. I saw Fransen and Tony Sellew riding off toward the XR together last night; this morning those four guns over there moved in—said Sellew had sent them out here to see we didn't have no more trouble. I don't like so damn many people so anxious to keep me out of trouble all of a sudden."

He saw the two hard lines appear at the corners of Dan Murdock's mouth, saw the trouble in the old man's eyes. Murdock said, "Sellew sent 'em out here?" He caught Ross's nod and exploded. "Hell, man! Lenore Warrington fired Tony Sellew two days ago. That's one thing made us change our mind, soon's we found out about it. If Tony Sellew sent those men he did it on his own!"

21

THEY KEPT it from the men at first, hoping against hope that it meant nothing. Both Ross and Murdock knew that something big was shaping up, but didn't know what move to make first to stop it. The men went to work, and the balance of the posts streamed up out of the canyon; the two wagons hauled them out to the end of the ever-growing fence line. Wire was strung, and hammers thudded staples into soggy posts. From time to time Ross glanced over toward where the four XR gunmen sat all day, playing cards under a rigged-up tarp. The last time he looked, he noticed that one of them was gone, and it was less than a half-hour later when they heard the shot.

Those who had heard it dropped their tools and stood there. Galt and Stuffy appeared from nowhere and took their places alongside Ross. Murdock's face grew suddenly older, more gray.

Ross spoke to Stuffy and Galt. "Let's go have a look-see. Maybe somebody just shot at a jack rabbit."

"Yeah," Galt said flatly.

They mounted horses and rode up the fence line toward the Saboba trail. When they came abreast the three XR gunmen the man called Rocky got up slowly and said, "Goin' some place, Parnell?"

"Just lookin' around," Ross said softly. "Thought we heard a shot."

"That so?" Rocky said, spitting out his cigarette. "Funny—I didn't hear nothing. Maybe you better get back to buildin' fence and forget it."

Ross's voice was low in his throat. He said, "I told you, we're looking around."

It was Galt who said, "Yeah, that's what he told yuh."

From the tail of his eye Ross saw that both Galt and Stuffy had six-shooters in their hands. He took the interval to draw his own gun. Rocky said, "Still handy with that thing, ain't you Galt?"

"Yeah," Galt said, grinning. "You and me was gonna have a contest some time, remember?"

"I'll wait until you ain't got a head start," Rocky said.

"Do that, Rocky. We're gonna scout around a little. We thought we heard a shot."

Rocky shrugged. "What the hell?" he said. "Sellew said I was to keep you away from Saboba. Long as you ain't goin' there I guess it will be all right. And you ain't goin' there. That's a long ways and you couldn't keep me covered all the time."

"Yeah, that's right, Rocky," Galt said. "You're too damn handy at bein' a dry gulcher."

"Glad you remember," Rocky said.

They rode on, Galt and Stuffy keeping back, their guns trained on Rocky and his men until they were out of six-shooter range. Then they spurred up alongside Ross. "You seem to know him right well," Ross said.

"Yeah." It was the only answer Galt offered.

They took the Saboba trail and rode slowly. "There's one man missing," Ross reminded them. "Maybe that's why Rocky was so easy on letting us go. I'll feel better when we're out in the open more."

"Maybe we've gone far enough," Stuffy said flatly. "Look there at the side of the trail."

They reined up and Ross saw the man sprawled out in the mud. There was a bright splotch of blood across the back of the head. At a little distance his horse stood, head drooped against the drizzling rain. They dismounted. Ross knelt beside the wounded man, felt for life, and found it. For a long time he just knelt there, trying to decide what it meant. After a while Galt said, "You know him?"

"Yes," Ross said. "I know him. Name of Sam Hedley."

"He was in a hell of a hurry to get some place," Stuffy said, running his hand across the sweat-caked hip of the riderless horse.

"And somebody was damn anxious he didn't get there,"

Ross said grimly, looking at the ugly scalp wound that had failed by a fraction of an inch to bring death.

"You're smart as hell, ain't you?" said a voice softly.

The three men turned and stared into the barrel of a 30/30 rifle gripped tightly in the hands of Rocky's missing XR gunman.

Ross muffled the instinct to make a try for his gun, forced his muscles to relax, and drawled, "What's the matter? Mad because we knocked off work?"

"Have a good time, funny boy," the gunman said, the expression on his face never changing. "You're Parnell, ain't you?"

"I'm popular as hell," Ross said dryly. "Want my coffin measurements?"

The gunman shook his head slightly. "I just hired on to kill you, not bury you."

It seemed to Ross that the man was listening, and in a few minutes Rocky and his two henchmen rode through the thicket and out onto the trail. Rocky had his perpetual grin. He said, "You didn't go far."

"Far enough to see you all in hell," said Ross. "We still call shootin' a man in the back of the head attempted murder hereabouts. Even Sheriff Yates would agree to that."

"It's attempted murder when somebody tells about it," Rocky corrected. One of the men had dismounted and was coming forward to relieve the men of their guns. Rocky said, "That short-set, ugly one—let him keep his. Him and me got a bet on."

"Thanks for nothin'," Galt said flatly.

A dozen-and-one thoughts raced through Ross's mind. These men were hired killers, completely impersonal. There seemed to be no possible opening. He said, "Mind if I smoke, Rocky?"

Rocky waited until his man had stepped in from behind, unbuckled Ross's gun belt and let it drop to the ground. Then he said, "Why not? Maybe you'll have a lot of smokin' to do where you're goin'."

Ross made the cigarette, and was surprised at the cool steadiness of his hands. While licking the paper he stole a glance at Stuffy and Galt. Stuffy was sucking thoughtfully on a tooth, as unconcerned as if he had been watching a card game. Except for the tenseness of the muscles along Galt's jaw there was little indication of emotion in the man. He seemed ready for any move that Rocky might make, even though he knew that his case was hopeless, satisfied as long as he was going to have a chance to go down shooting.

Ross's hand started toward his shirt pocket for a match and a gun smacked against his spine. He stood frozen for a second, then said, "I usually light my cigarettes before I smoke 'em."

Rocky laughed—a short, hard laugh. "Go ahead," he said.

Ross drew the smoke deeply into his lungs, glanced up at Rocky, and said, "Mind telling me what the hell it's all about before you shoot me?"

The gunman shrugged. "How the hell do I know?" he said. "I don't ask questions. When Fransen and Sellew get to hell, ask them."

"I meant Hedley here," Ross said, keeping his voice emotionless. "Who the hell did he cross up?"

"Ask him," Rocky suggested. "How do you want it, in the back or in the gut? That don't go for you, Galt. I want to see you try to get that slick gun out after you got a couple of slugs in you. It's been a long time."

"You ain't changed none, Rocky," said Galt.

The others were off their horses now; they had drawn their guns and cocked them. The tall, skinny one with splotches of freckles on his hands picked Ross for a target. They moved around in a straight line closer to the bushes, making a mock ceremony out of it.

The tall, skinny one lined his gun on Ross's middle. Ross felt the perspiration standing out on his upper lip, running off his forehead; the man with the gun grinned wickedly. Then suddenly, without any warning, he took a step forward, arching his back awkwardly; he seemed to fumble with the gun, then his fingers stiffened, and the weapon dropped to the ground. He started to curse, and a bloody froth bubbled across his lips. He took two more steps, fell, twisted grotesquely, one hand going toward his back. There was a knife sticking between his shoulder blades.

Before there was another move, a shotgun blasted twice. Two of Rocky's men seemed to rise out of their tracks, blown half in two by the load of buckshot. In that split second Galt moved for his gun.

The first of Galt's bullets thudded into the pommel of Rocky's saddle. Rocky threw himself to one side, his gun spurting death, and Ross saw Galt go down, rolling. On the other side of him Stuffy fired once. Rocky's gun blazed again, then Galt had him in his sights. He fired twice more. The last shot caught Rocky as he was falling out of the saddle.

Morales came out of the bushes first, his white teeth exposed in a hideous grin, a knife gripped in his hand. They heard the click of a shotgun breaking, then Chico pushed his way through the brush, shoving two new shells into that murderous weapon. The little Mexican grinned and said, "When we see these hombres come this way we theenk we better follow. That good for you, no?"

Ross could have sworn there were tears in his eyes. He looked at the little Mexican, felt a grin he was having trouble controlling tug at his lips. He said, "That good for us, yes!"

22

SAM HEDLEY came to, fighting. It took them a good five minutes to convince him where he was, and then he didn't calm down until he saw Ross. Galt, who had received a slight hip wound, was sitting there in the rain, smoking a cigarette while Stuffy methodically probed for a bullet. He winced and said, "That old turkey's got a lot of gravel in his craw."

Sam said, "These friends of yours, Ross?"

"Every one of them," said Ross.

"Then you better get set. Fransen and Sellew are plannin' on blastin' hell out of the whole valley."

"How'd you find out, Sam?"

Sam Hedley looked a bit sheepish. "That girl in the saloon—that Queenie. I went off half cocked again, I reckon. I figgered she had something to do with Bret gettin' mixed up in this thing; I went in there after her. I don't know what I figgered on doin'—maybe I was gonna kill her. She told me after that Warrington woman fired Sellew he come in there drunk and roarin' mad. He'd been tellin' Queenie he was gonna marry her, I guess."

"What about Fransen?" Ross demanded.

Sam touched his scalp and winced. "I'm comin' to that, damn it. The gal said him and Sellew got together and Fransen said somethin' about why be satisfied with half a pie. Next thing she knowed she got to talkin' to Tony about gettin' married, and he slapped hell out of her— called her a bunch of names and told her to get the hell out of town; him and Fransen had pitched in together. Sellew took what crew he could count on and went down to the XR. He's got that Miz Warrington there and aims to hold out against all comers. Fransen figgers long as these other fellers are out here buildin' fence he'll make a sweep on their places and raise so much hell they'll never be able to pay off them mortgages he holds. Then him and Sellew can divvy up and we can all go whistle up a stump. They been tryin' to keep you out of town until they could get set."

Ross didn't hear the rest of what Sam had to say. He mentally counted the men he had here and realized that, splitting them to send half to the XR and half to protect their own places, he'd have nothing. He said suddenly, "Warrington and those farmers still in town?"

"Was when I left," Sam said.

Ross shot a quick order to Murdock, then said, "I'm going for some more help."

Murdock said, "You're crazy, man. Suppose you run into Fransen and his gang?"

"I'll take that chance," Ross said.

He glanced over the horses quickly, picked the best-looking one in the lot, and told old Gomez to saddle it. He threw himself into the saddle, sank his spurs, and the horse streaked out across the soggy mesa.

The fear in him grew to monstrous proportions as he headed back toward town. The impatience in him was a thing he couldn't put off, and he took a short-cut trail through the breaks, cutting through by Ed Tozier's. He rode only close enough to the house to see that it was a mass of flame.

A thousand thoughts raced through Ross's mind. Practically every able-bodied man on these places had ridden out, or was on the way out to help him build a fence. He felt a crazy, half-mad fear as he thought of Judge Iverson and Jean and Maria. He was cursing like a madman, all sense and reason gone from him, when he pounded across the bridge and rode into Saboba.

He found Herbert Warrington at the general merchandise store and wasted little time trying to reason with the man. The wheat farmers were there, a half dozen of them. They stood back in a half-circle, grim-faced, ready to come to Warrington's assistance if he needed them.

Ross gripped Warrington's shirt front and shook him. He said, "She's done everything but come crawling on her hands and knees to you. Get out there now and show her you're a man."

He left and rode over to Iverson's, and the savage strength that was in him ran out, leaving him weak with relief when he saw that everything was all right there. Without realizing what he was doing, he took Jean in his arms, held her close, and kissed her hungrily. He said, "Your dad's all right, Jean. He's all right, all the way through."

She seemed to know what he meant.

He said, "They've already been to Tozier's. They'll head for Palomar's next. I'll try to get out there and warn Diego."

She clung to him for only a second, and then let him go. He rode his jaded horse back to the center of town, jumped free of the saddle, and took the first fresh horse he saw at the hitch rail. He saw Herbert Warrington and his wheat farmers running on foot toward the livery stable at the end of the street; then his spurs drew blood, and he was headed back out of town in the direction of the Palomar place.

In less than a mile he had picked up the trail of the raiders. It was not a hard trail to follow; they had made no effort to cover it up. They were heading straight across the gently rolling, unfenced ground toward Tozier's. From there it was only a matter of a few miles to Palomar's, then a short stretch of open country to Murdock's. He could only pray now that Murdock and the fence crew would intercept them before they had gone too far.

He caught up with them finally, but it was too late to do anything about saving Diego Palomar's house. He kept thinking of Diego's waxlike wife, and hoping that some miracle had let her escape. He paused only long enough to make sure his gun was ready, and then rode straight in toward where Ben Fransen's rustler band and hired Hogtown killers were circling the place. It sickened him to see the blood lust of this crew.

They rode like a band of Apaches, shooting at anything and everything. He saw a chicken cut across the barnyard, saw a man fire, and saw the chicken tumble end over end. A dog went yelping out from the barn, and a shot caught it and rolled it. Ruthless, needless destruction by power-crazy men who had been promised a slice of an empire. He saw Ben Fransen, sitting his horse to one side, watching it all with satisfaction; Ross yelled, his voice hoarse and cracking. "All right, Fransen! You got guts enough to make this man to man?"

There was only a second's hesitation on the part of Ben Fransen. It would have been useless for him to call for help, because his men were too bent on their destruction. Ross saw him fight his horse, reach for the gun in his waistband, and then Fransen was riding straight toward him and his gun was blazing death.

Ross felt lead sear across his ribs, knocking him half out of the saddle. Then he had his sight lined on that massive chest and he pulled the trigger. He didn't have a chance to see Ben Fransen go down, didn't know whether or not he had killed him, for a dozen riders, seeing the fight, had turned and closed in around him.

His hat went sailing off his head and he felt like someone had dumped a bucket of scalding water down his neck. He clutched at the saddlehorn, barely managing to hang onto his six-shooter. Something smashed against his arm, and he went out of the saddle. Hoofs cut the mud around his face. He lay there, not daring to move. Then he heard the sound of new guns, the wild yell of

men, and he knew that Dan Murdock and the fence builders had joined the fight.

It was a wild welter of slaughter then; bullets at first,
and then men clubbing men with guns; close shots that
smelled up the air with the stench of burning cloth and
seared flesh; screams and curses. Ross tried to get into it,
and found that he couldn't make it, so he gradually edged
his way out of danger and lay there against the side of
a shed panting, trying to stop the blood that streamed
from the slight flesh wound in his left arm.

He fought his way to his feet, still dizzy from the blow
he had received in the head. He stood there, swaying,
and saw Dan Murdock, a gun in his hand, backing three
men with hands high against the side of the barn. Chico
was there, and Morales, apparently unhurt. He tried to
spot Stuffy and couldn't and then he saw old Gomez,
strutting with importance.

Diego Palomar and his own crew came in then. He
could hear them talking excitedly to Dan Murdock. They
had started for the fence line, heard the shots, and turned
back, too late to get into the actual fight but in time to
round up a few stragglers. It wasn't until then that Ross
thought of Trip Levitt. He couldn't recall having seen
him in the fight.

He started making his way down toward the barn and
he came to the place where Ben Fransen's body lay in
the mud. A dozen horses had passed over it and it was
broken and smashed beyond recognition. It made Ross
sick to his stomach.

One of the men found Palomar's wife, hysterical, un-
consolable. She had seen the riders coming and had gone
to a small coulee a half mile from the house and hidden
there. From that point she had witnessed the slaughter.
Don Diego took her in his arms and he kept saying, "My
paloma—my pobre paloma."

Ross said, "Diego, you stay here with your wife. We'll leave three other men with you. Lock this crew up in the barn and keep an eye on them until someone can talk Sheriff Yates into doing something about them. The rest of us are going on down to the XR. There's trouble there too."

Dan Murdock said, "You're not going any place, Ross. Look at you."

Ross said, "If somebody will tie up this wing it will be all right—just a scratch. I've got a personal stand in this fight, and I haven't run into it yet."

He fought against the delay, but they made him wait until they could wash and bandage the wound, making sure it wasn't dangerous. Then they got some coffee and food into his belly and afterward, riding at an easy lope toward the XR, he was glad they had made him do it.

He had no idea what size crew Tony Sellew might have at the XR headquarters. If Sellew chose to hold out from inside that fortresslike house he could stand off an army. It was only speculation as to how much of a fight Warrington and his wheat ranchers could make, if they had come here at all.

By the time they had topped the rise that looked down on the gigantic strength of old Tuck Brant's XR fortress, Ross's body was a solid block of pain, and there was only room for one clear thought in his mind—Trip Levitt.

23

THEY REINED UP there on that little rise of ground, and looked down on the sprawling headquarters ranch, with its solid barn and the double post-hole corrals, and the huge, blocky U of the house itself. They could see the dozen saddled horses still there in the corral and even from here they could recognize the white-stockinged bay of Tony Sellew tied there in that courtyard that had once been a flower garden. There was no sign of Herbert Warrington and his wheat ranchers.

They waited then, better than half an hour, knowing they were within full sight of the men in that house, knowing there was small chance of breaking through. Ross walked up and down, working the stiffness out of his legs, fighting the pain in his punctured left arm.

Old Gomez built a small fire and heated a canteen of brackish water that had been left hanging on one of the saddles in a dryer day. He removed the bandage from Ross's arm, washed the wound, and soaked the cloth with the warm water, then rebandaged it. The warmth brought a little relief.

Somebody had a bottle of whisky in one of the saddle-bags and started passing it around. It burned like fire, but, temporarily at least, it stimulated their circulation.

The afternoon dragged on with killing, deadening monotony; the big house down there seemed to smirk at them as each man made a plan and had it rejected—the house that Tuck Brant had built; the house that could never be taken. A thick, futile hopelessness touched all of them, and tempers became short and words harsh, and questions went unanswered.

And then near evening they came. A long string of men: thirty of them, perhaps, maybe more, coming not from the direction of Saboba, but straight across the endless, undulating plain from the breaks of the Catclaw, from the land that lay between that river and the escarpment—the land of wheat.

There was only one man in this country who rode a Tennessee walking horse with a postage-stamp saddle—Herbert Warrington; he had a rifle gripped tightly in his right hand.

The rest were solid, blocky men—men of the soil, riding mules, riding work horses, As they came nearer, Ross could make out a half-dozen buckboards jogging across the sea of grass. Gomez said softly, "Thees is why he did not come before—he go to get every farmer in the country."

So now it was war, with that long, unbroken line moving in relentlessly from the east, and Ross Parnell and his faster-moving body of fighting men here on the knoll to the west. They could squeeze in from both sides now, or from the front and the back, or they could completely surround the place. But still there would be no breaking through those impregnable walls that Tuck Brant had built for just such an emergency. And inside those walls Ross knew Lenore Brant Warrington was trapped, just as all her life she had been trapped by her father's dictates and by his desires.

He motioned for his men to mount and ride wide out of gun range to meet Herbert Warrington and figure out a plan.

The thing that impressed Ross when he was near Warrington was the indomitable determination of the man. It was the same thing he had noticed the first time he had met Warrington back at the south fence in a time that seemed ages ago. It was the thing that had made him decide Warrington had the power within him to push a thing to completion once it was started. It was the thing that overshadowed what weakness there was in Warrington's face and now completely concealed the actual slightness of his body. Warrington shifted the rifle to his left hand and he offered his right hand, stiffly, formally. He said only, "Is she in there, Parnell?"

Ross nodded. "As far as I know."

"Then we'll get her out before we start anything," said Warrington. He said it as if it were already an accomplished fact.

Ross saw the farmer and son he had met at the bar that night at Jim East's and nodded to them. The old man said, "We brung powder and fuse."

"Get it set," Warrington said. "I'm going after her."

"Are you crazy, man?" Ross said, his voice high-pitched.

Warrington shook his head. "I have been for some time. I'm not now. There's a window there in the east wing. I put it in myself. She'll be there. I'll get her out that way. You take your men and join mine and keep them busy at the front of the house until I give the signal that she's safe."

Ross could begin to see now what Lenore had seen in this man and he could see how it was that her love for him had grown as fiercely strong as it had. He said, "I'll go with you, Warrington."

Warrington said, "You don't need to, Parnell."

Ross said, "I know that. I'll go."

They looked at each other; in that moment they were friends and they knew it, and it would take a lot to break that friendship. They rode with the others, and when they came to the lane of cottonwoods, they dropped out of formation there and kept themselves screened. While the rest of the band rode on toward the front of the house they dismounted. They said nothing as they crouched there behind the cottonwoods. They could hear the horses and the buckboards drawing up in formation, and the orders of men passing up and down the line.

And then it came, the first volley of rifle fire—a long, rippling sound like a line of cavalry drawn up in action. They could hear the smack of lead against the adobe walls, then the answering fire from within the house. After that, it was a steady roar of gunfire, and their nostrils flared as the tang of burnt powder caught in the wind and drifted even there. Warrington jerked his head, and together they started moving from one cottonwood to the next, making their way up the long line of trees to where the leaden sheen of the afternoon sky reflected itself in the big glass window in the east wing of the house.

The battle in front seemed to increase in intensity. A useless fight, they both knew. A senseless exchange of lead by men out of range of the gunfire from within the house, men who poured an endless fire into the impregnable walls of Tuck Brant's citadel. But as long as it continued, Ross and Warrington could move here undetected, and they forced their way closer and closer, until at last they were flattened there, breathing heavily, against the side of the east wing of the house.

They paused only for seconds to catch their breath, then, running low, they came to the big window and with one swift movement Warrington's rifle butt crashed against the solid sheet of glass.

It splintered out with a crash that was not completely concealed by the gunfire and Warrington called her name. She came running to the broken window. First she said, "Thank God you're all right;" then she ran back to the hall door and grabbed at the arm of Chang, the old Chinaman who stood with a meat cleaver in his hand.

They helped Lenore and Chang over the low sill and down onto the ground. And for a long second Warrington and his wife stood there, locked in each other's arms, their lips pressed together in a long kiss. It was Chang who called the warning. The doorway to the hall had slammed open and Trip Levitt and Tony Sellew stood there. They had guns in their hands.

There was only time to knock Lenore and the Chinaman to the ground and then Warrington had his rifle to his shoulder and was firing through the broken glass. An unexplainable instinct told Ross that Warrington had picked Sellew for his target.

And now, as Ross finally saw Trip Levitt coming toward him, he seemed to have an eternity in which to savor the impact of the moment. He could see that broad, flat nose set between beady eyes. The hard, cruel mouth, the cleft in the flat chin. Even over the roar of Warrington's rifle he could distinctly hear Trip Levitt say, "It's been a long time, Parnell." And then both men fired. There was an eternity that must have been less than a tenth of a second—an eternity in which a gun bucked against the palm of his hand and drove out every remnant of a past that had made him a drifter and twisted his thoughts. The haze of the gunsmoke cleared in front of his eyes and he saw Trip Levitt's knees bending, sagging out from under him. Then the big man fell and was out of sight below the low sill of the window.

They ran then, Herbert Warrington and Ross Parnell, taking Lenore and the Chinaman with them. They ran until the breath screamed from Ross's lungs and he didn't know why they ran. Until finally they threw themselves flat on the ground and he heard Warrington yell, saw him wave his hand, and then he knew.

There was a horrible earth-shaking explosion. The entire center of the big house seemed to give way. Sticks and glass and debris sprayed up in a huge, spouting, smoke-crested mushroom, then came cascading down; the echo of the blast rolled out across the prairie, spreading in ever-widening ripples, rolling north toward Saboba, south toward the long fence and the wheatlands, east to the Catclaw.

Ross turned then, and saw that Herbert Warrington was holding Lenore in his arms. She was crying softly. He saw that she was wearing a dress.

The only thing left of the XR ranch house was the long east wing, and in that were the bodies of two dead men.

The kitchen was in that wing too, and after some of the men had taken out Sellew and Levitt, Chang went back to his stove and his pots and pans as if nothing had happened. They set up a long table in the floored part of the barn, and Chico and Morales went with the Chinaman to dish out the steaming kettles of food. It was Stuffy who gave Herbert Warrington a hand with the case of whisky. He looked at Ross, grinned, and said, "Galt will be sore as hell when he finds out what he missed."

They ate and drank there at that long table: Lenore and Herbert Warrington, owners of a cattle kingdom; broad-handed, hard-faced men who were turning the plains into an empire of wheat; and the crews of the small ranches north of the Sasinaw—ranches that would never grow big, but would always be a part of this country.

But Ross was anxious to get away from it now, and it was not the old urge to drift that had always been so strong in him. He fretted and stewed and twisted uneasily on the bench until Lenore came and laid her hand on his arm, saying, "Why don't you go see her before it kills you?"

Ross felt himself flushing deeply. He looked up and saw that Herbert Warrington was laughing at him. Warrington said, "My wife's advice is good in such things, Ross. Better listen to it."

Ross saw that several other of the men were grinning broadly now. He got up awkwardly, took his hat, and started to leave the table. Warrington got up and went with him outside the barn.

As they stood there in the fast-gathering darkness the clouds rolled on south, and the new-washed sky was heavy with stars. Warrington said softly, "It's all over, Ross. The past and all of it. Come to see us often, will you?"

"I'll do that, Herb," Ross said.

He mounted his horse then and rode north, toward Saboba. He kept thinking of Jean and how once she had asked him if he ever made plans about anything and he had told her no. He kept hoping now she would ask him that same question again. He'd have a different answer.

THE END

"REACH FOR THE SKY!"

and you still won't find more excitement or more thrills than you get in Bantam's slam-bang, action-packed westerns! Here's a roundup of fast-reading stories by some of America's greatest western writers:

☐	14207	**WARRIOR'S PATH** Louis L'Amour	$1.95
☐	13651	**THE STRONG SHALL LIVE** Louis L'Amour	$1.95
☐	13781	**THE IRON MARSHAL** Louis L'Amour	$1.95
☐	14219	**OVER ON THE DRY SIDE** Louis L'Amour	$1.95
☐	14196	**SACKETT** Louis L'Amour	$1.95
☐	13838	**TROUBLE COUNTRY** Luke Short	$1.75
☐	13679	**CORONER CREEK** Luke Short	$1.75
☐	14185	**PONY EXPRESS** Gary McCarthy	$1.75
☐	14475	**SHANE** Jack Schaefer	$1.95
☐	14179	**GUNSMOKE GRAZE** Peter Dawson	$1.75
☐	14178	**THE CROSSING** Clay Fisher	$1.75
☐	13696	**LAST STAND AT SABER RIVER** Elmore Leonard	$1.75
☐	12888	**GUNSIGHTS** Elmore Leonard	$1.50
☐	10727	**OUTLAW** Frank Gruber	$1.50

Buy them at your local bookstore or use this handy coupon for ordering:

BANTAM'S #1
ALL-TIME BESTSELLING AUTHOR
AMERICA'S FAVORITE WESTERN WRITER

☐	13561	THE STRONG SHALL LIVE	$1.95
☐	12354	BENDIGO SHAFTER	$2.25
☐	13881	THE KEY-LOCK MAN	$1.95
☐	13719	RADIGAN	$1.95
☐	13609	WAR PARTY	$1.95
☐	13882	KIOWA TRAIL	$1.95
☐	13683	THE BURNING HILLS	$1.95
☐	14762	SHALAKO	$2.25
☐	14881	KILRONE	$2.25
☐	13794	THE RIDER OF LOST CREEK	$1.95
☐	13798	CALLAGHEN	$1.95
☐	14114	THE QUICK AND THE DEAD	$1.95
☐	14219	OVER ON THE DRY SIDE	$1.95
☐	13722	DOWN THE LONG HILLS	$1.95
☐	14316	WESTWARD THE TIDE	$1.95
☐	14227	KID RODELO	$1.95
☐	14104	BROKEN GUN	$1.95
☐	13898	WHERE THE LONG GRASS BLOWS	$1.95
☐	14411	HOW THE WEST WAS WON	$1.95

Buy them at your local bookstore or use this
handy coupon for ordering:

LUKE SHORT
BEST-SELLING WESTERN WRITER

Luke Short's name on a book guarantees fast-action stories and color-
ful characters which mean slam-bang reading as in these Bantam
editions:

☐ 13679	CORONER CREEK	$1.75
☐ 13585	DONOVAN'S GUN	$1.75
☐ 12380	SILVER ROCK	$1.50
☐ 14176	FEUD AT SINGLE SHOT	$1.75
☐ 14181	PAPER SHERIFF	$1.75
☐ 13834	RIDE THE MAN DOWN	$1.75
☐ 13760	DESERT CROSSING	$1.75
☐ 12634	VENGEANCE VALLEY	$1.50
☐ 14183	WAR ON THE CIMARRON	$1.75
☐ 12385	THE SOME-DAY COUNTRY	$1.50

Bantam Book Catalog

Here's your up-to-the-minute listing of over 1,400 titles by your favorite authors.

This illustrated, large format catalog gives a description of each title. For your convenience, it is divided into categories in fiction and non-fiction—gothics, science fiction, westerns, mysteries, cookbooks, mysticism and occult, biographies, history, family living, health, psychology, art.

So don't delay—take advantage of this special opportunity to increase your reading pleasure.

Just send us your name and address and 50¢ (to help defray postage and handling costs).